LOVE IS THE WINNER

LOVE IS THE WINNER

JANET TEMPLETON

Doubleday

NEW YORK

1988

ROM
F
TEM

Library of Congress Cataloging-in-Publication Data
Templeton, Janet, 1926–
Love is the winner/Janet Templeton.—1st ed.
p.   cm.
"Starlight romance"—P.
I. Title.
PS3558.E78L595   1988
813'.54—dc19   87-25049
CIP
ISBN 0-385-24341-3

Once more, for
Veronica Mixon

LOVE IS THE WINNER

CHAPTER ONE

Cressida Fleet was permitting her eyes to rest briefly on the figure of a handsome young man striding to the enclosure at the far end of this racetrack. She derived a feeling of innocent pleasure from this lull on the warm June afternoon.

The few moments of peace were concluded by an urgent interruption.

"My dear," said Mrs. Fleet, having approached from a northerly direction and come to roost at her daughter's left. The good lady looked irritable for once. "The next race is to begin shortly and you appear to have accomplished nothing whatever."

Recalled to another consideration of important matters, Cressida made an admission.

"I am uncertain about the prowess of Lover's Knot."

"Then we miss the chance to wager on this day's biggest race," Mrs. Fleet pointed out.

Her objection was well taken. The Fleets, mother and daughter, father and son, had not ventured out to Cheshire for the pleasure of boating on the admirable River Dee. Mr. and Mrs. Fleet and their progeny had embarked on this *hegira* from London in the pursuit of financial gain. The goal was proving unwontedly elusive.

"I suppose we must wager on this one," Cressida said hesitantly.

Mr. Hartley Fleet, the paterfamilias of his clan, had approached on Cressida's other side. He was shaking his head a little sadly.

"We have had an insufficient return on the day's other races and one successful wager will be of great use," he said.

Cressida nodded at her father. Papa must have been considered a handsome young man, she thought, not for the first time as she looked directly at him. Even now, he wore a straw boater,

Norfolk jacket, and dark striped trousers as though he had been poured into them by someone with a steady hand.

"If we must wager," Cressida pointed out, "it is possible to take the odds."

"Any return on such a wager would be too small to justify our investment."

Mrs. Fleet suggeted, "We can bet the field bar one, of course."

Cressida shook her head urgently. She was a firm nonbeliever in betting on the entire field less one steed or two or three. In her experience it was just those animals who had been excluded that were most likely to come surging to the post ahead of the others.

And it can be said that her experience was wide. Since the halcyon days of youth, when Mr. Fleet had unwittingly introduced her to the joys of racing as seen by spectators and bettors, she had unhesitatingly taken to the sport. From the age of thirteen she had been able to assert, correctly as it nearly always turned out, that a certain horse would race ill on flat terrain, another would take well to a six-stone handicap, a third would perform badly at a course with sharp turns. No one in the family knew from whence the gift had sprung, unless it had been inherited from the father of Mr. Fleet, a man with an almost unnatural ability to capitalize upon the gyrations of the stock market. The Fleet family were impressed one and all by Cressida's abilities.

The gift had been seriously called into play only a short time after the moneys inherited from Mr. Fleet's father had finally been expended. The family had faced the likelihood of penury.

It was Torin, Cressida's older brother, who first remembered the skill that his sister had somehow acquired, and considered applying it liberally to the problem under discussion.

"Cressida can earn money by telling us which horses to bet upon."

"I would not consent," Mr. Fleet had demurred, "to so harebrained a scheme."

Whereupon his good wife promptly remarked, "Our first requirement is survival."

Cressida had immediately been pressed into service as a Nostradamus of the race meetings. It was a situation with great advantages to the family. They traveled in the season, and did themselves as well as they pleased. Further, they retained many friends among the Sociables. None of these could have been aware of the depths to which the Fleet family had been lowered or the heights to which they had risen, depending on the vantage point of an abstainer or a gambler.

For Cressida, however, despite the advantages, there was a price to be paid.

While her friends were in pursuit of husbands, she was most likely at the races for purposes of bettering the family income. When balls were taking place, she was at home checking the statements in sporting papers about the skills of various horses and jockeys. If ever she was attracted by a young man, her family could not help looking askance. Even the most generous of the Fleets was likely to blanch at the thought of a good income going by the boards because of sundry rituals of mating.

During the fall and winter, when racing was of no concern to any but breeders, Cressida felt that she occupied much of her time apologizing to friends for not having been observed beyond the boundaries of racetracks during the height of the past season. Those others probably felt that the Fleets young and old were fanatic on the one subject, not realizing the necessity for such close attention to the Sport of Kings.

Cressida, as a result, found herself with precious little experience in the art and craft of dealing with men who might otherwise have been induced by her comeliness and intelligence to make an offer for her. At the age of seventeen, the lovely young blonde already contemplated, in her less optimistic moments, a future with no men in her life except father and brother and no interest in any other male who didn't have four legs.

Within limits, it may therefore be understood by way of summary of the cogent facts, Cressida Fleet was a happy young woman. In June of 1897, however, at the time when our account commences, the limits were assuming an ever greater importance in her life.

Cressida was looking around her in order to make certain that none of the racing crowd of Sociables were within earshot. Any apprehension along those lines was momentarily unfounded. Those who were not in the enclosure overlooking the finish line at the oval track were at the other end, where an irregular circle contained various turf accountants in the act of accepting wagers. Except for members of the Fleet family, there was hardly a bouffant sleeve or a straw boater to be seen.

She nodded at her brother, who was approaching at an easy speed that would have done credit to some good horse already far ahead of the field. Torin, like her father in his youth, was a handsome young man with a firm chin below the finely drawn Fleet features. He required only the most cursory glance before comprehending the nature of the current difficulty.

"Cress, what can we do to help you make up your mind about the starters?"

"Only one horse is causing me a problem and that is Lover's Knot," she explained.

"He ran badly at the St. Leger last season," Torin said after a swift glance at the racing paper in his right hand. The information he offered was already known to her. "Is that any part of your difficulty?"

There was no time for protracted discussion.

"I must see the horses parade to the starting line, at any rate, it may be of use." It was a custom of hers not to agree that any bet be made until she had inspected the field so as to judge the spirits in which horses were entering a fray.

As if for the first time, Mr. Fleet grumbled, "That will leave us the fewest moments to notify individual bookies of our preference."

Mrs. Fleet stirred, causing a bouffant sleeve to rustle in the brief updraft. She was wearing wool with a pearl-gray velvet scarf on each shoulder and a high collar with turned-over points in front. As ever, she was perfectly turned out, displaying a skill she had not yet been able to pass along to her daughter.

"We will walk down to the rail where you can see more clearly," said Gladys Fleet with a businesslike toss of her bonneted head. "I feel sure it won't take too long for you to reach a proper decision. It never does. . . . Why, Cressida, what is the matter all of a sudden? Why do you look so?"

"I? Oh, no reason, Mama, none at all."

She had needed a moment to recover her bearings after taking in the sight of a young man leaving the enclosure, the same handsome one she had previously observed. He was tall, with an imperial nose and strong features that testified to an outdoor roughness which she found refreshing. His stride had a decisiveness that would have shamed her brother. In a world of perfumed geldings, this man was obviously—but she refrained from concluding that thought and supposed she was blushing to the roots of her blond hair.

It seemed to Cressida that he would shortly be finding himself at the rear of the premises. If she put on a burst of speed, it would be possible to encounter him if only for a moment, to smile and perhaps speak a word or two and hear him speak in return. She did not yet know about the timbre of his voice, although she suspected it would prove resonant. The family would not interfere, as they were likely to deduce that she was searching for information about the particular four-footed animal whose previous antics had been a source of disturbance to her.

A look downward as she moved caused her to feel satisfied at her costume on this day. She was wearing wool tinted with persian lilacs, and felt that they accented the bright blue of her eyes, as did the bishop's mantle of fuzzy molleton. Her collar flared as she accelerated her pace and she could feel the rustle of Neapolitan braid on her bonnet. She might have rigged herself out to even better effect had she known that she would see so striking a male, but she was not (as has been said) wholly unhappy with her appearance.

The gentleman's stride was of such a velocity that he might very well escape her.

Cressida considered such a prospect to be less than bearable. A young woman with greater experience in these matters might have offered a shy smile or widened her astonishingly attractive eyes. Cressida took a more direct path. Deftly utilizing her closed parasol of white chiffon mousseline, she angled it below the nearest knee of the gentleman in motion.

The results would have pleased the most self-critical of mortals. The gentleman had been walking ahead with splendid confidence, but now he wavered. A frown crossed those rugged features at the concept of any part of his body suddenly refusing to do what had been ordered. He swayed like a tree in a thunderstorm. Where his form had been occupying space only a moment before, there was suddenly nothing to be seen other than the surrounding area. It would have been palpable to an intelligence far meaner than Cressida's that the gentleman had lost his balance and fallen.

Conscience-stricken at long last, she rushed forward to be of assistance. It was an unladylike gesture. A frown of scorn crossed the gentleman's face. He restored his balance without aid.

Seen from a closer vantage, it became even clearer that the skin of his face had blessedly been tempered and roughened by the outdoors and not by strong drink. Under the varicolored jacket and rainbow tie and white shirt there did not appear to be an ounce of superfluous weight. If Cressida had ordered a gentleman to her specifications, he would have resembled this one in every external feature.

He had briefly been examining the source of his downfall. A glint in those astonishing eyes of his, light gray and with irises of a similar shading, gave mute but strong testimony to his aesthetic satisfaction with her appearance.

Cressida would not pretend that no incident had taken place between them.

"I owe you an apology, I fear," she began.

Only the crisp June air was suddenly receiving her confidences, not the gentleman at all. He had given an irritable shake of the head and glanced at his turnip-sized pocket watch, then turned and loped to the railing.

In this latter gesture he was not alone. Sociables of both sexes, dressed in peacock finery to attend the racing, had taken the same path. Clearly the parade of horses to the starting line was within moments of getting under way.

Cressida had no intention of losing sight of this male, nor would she forego the necessary duty of inspecting the horses. Happily, she could accomplish both tasks. With the family walking firmly at her back, she embarked upon the twin labors.

Her human quarry had been halted for some brief conversation with another of his species. The latter, more roughly costumed than most of the patrons, suddenly smiled and touched Cressida's quarry on a shoulder before leaving. It was a motion that the gentleman did not shrug off. Cressida was unaware of any reason for such a display, and gave no thought to the matter. She was just as pleased that her quarry had not disappeared into the thick of the crowd.

Only when he looked sideways at her did it faintly occur to Cressida that she ought to have feigned surprise at seeing him yet again. By that time, of course, it was far too late.

"I do owe you an apology, I fear."

She was on the point of adding untruthfully that the recent contretemps had been caused by a regrettable and wholly inexplicable accident. The lie offered some compromise in the direction of graciousness, but the words seemed stuck in her throat and would not make themselves heard.

Whatever form an excuse might have taken suddenly became moot. The gentleman leaned forward in the direction of the railing.

The procession had begun.

There is a craft to the inspection of horses prior to a race, as Cressida had learned in the youthful stages of her career. One of the animals might be in a fractious mood for whatever reason, negligible to a human but of great importance to a noble equine. Another could suddenly be torpid. The careful observer, bringing every known resource of intelligence into play, must be alert to those signs that show themselves and as a result bestow his patronage, so to speak, upon a rival.

"Ah!" she said as the horses moved along the moist grass-bordered oval to the starting point. Having noted the colors in which individual jockeys were swathed and being therefore able to identify varied horses, she was speaking more to herself than anyone else. "My first judgment was correct. Scapegrace is the horse."

The gentleman surprised Cressida and perhaps himself by turning in her direction. He looked angry.

"Are you so misguided as to think that Scapegrace could possibly win?" he paused. "One can expect no less from a wealthy dilettante."

Cressida did not offer any correction to this appraisal of her position in life. She had achieved the goal of speaking with him, but it had become apparent that his opinion of her was not the one that she wanted to encourage. She had succeeded, but found herself realizing that at the same time she had failed dismally.

CHAPTER TWO

Cressida was now torn by conflicting desires. On the one hand she wanted to remain silent while in propinquity to this male. At the same time, she wanted to know whether he could muster any information whatever to reinforce what might have been a mere prejudice against one horse and in favor of another. Because her family was nearby and waiting for direct word from the fount of wisdom she had become on racing matters, she chose to engage him in further verbal swordplay.

"Lover's Knot is headstrong," she pointed out, shifting the argument from a statement without substance. "He tosses every possible part of his body on the way to start a race. No jockey will be able to manage him in the field, not for a moment."

His next look in her direction was different from any that had preceded it. Cressida formed the distinct impression that he was stirred by her ability to offer a reason for the decision she had made, however tentative she considered it.

"Your ladyship," he said sarcastically, alluding to her as someone with considerable money. It was gall and wormwood for Cressida to discover that his voice was a pleasant baritone. "If you plan to throw out money on Scapegrace, let me at least point out, perhaps needlessly, that he moves in a flat-footed manner. It is a certain sign of a poor race to follow."

"Flat-footedly, yes, but with speed and with his head erect, an indicator that no other horse can possibly match. Need I remind you in turn what Lover's Knot did in last year's St. Leger Classic at Doncaster?"

"I am well aware of what took place on the painful occasion, which you so gracefully recall to me." The pleasant baritone was suddenly higher in timbre edged by hoarfrost. "Lover's Knot consolidated his position before the finish of the race."

"What you are saying is that he propped," Cressida reminded him sternly. "Lover's Knot propped on the track in mid-race."

"No, I disagree. It looked that way, I suppose."

"According to the *Racing Intelligencer*, he stuck his forelegs into the dirt just as Pommes Frites was gaining on him."

"He was being ill-handled by a jockey who had no appreciation of a high-spirited beauty."

"For whatever reason, the horse propped."

He shrugged his shoulders massively, neither giving in on the point nor disputing it any further.

"Your ladyship can bet on any horse she chooses, of course. Bet on Persimmon, if you like, even though he is not in the race."

"If the Prince of Wales's horse was in this race, no one would bet on any other, if only in consideration of Persimmon having won last season's Derby." She turned to her family. "Scapegrace it is."

The men left to place their wagers with different turf accountants. Mama, seeing that Cressida remained in place, chose to stay some two-and-a-half lengths away. Any further conversation between Cressida and her tormentor would be unclear to her. Not that Cressida had the least intention of discoursing further with the man, handsome and strong-voiced and self-assured though he was.

He suddenly said, "If you are so confident about the beast you endorse, then you should not hesitate to make a subsidiary wager *à deux*, so to speak."

A while ago she would have been pleased by an offer that would connote seeing more of the handsome one. Time had worked its spell in reverse, however. She told herself that she would rather have made a bet with one of the horses.

"Thank you, but I never indulge privately for money."

"No, I suppose that might be unseemly." He had apparently fixed the idea in his mind that Cressida Fleet was a female of prodigious wealth. "Though you can certainly afford to do so, I am sure."

She chose not to correct him. Indeed she stood with her nose slightly elevated, as if to convey that she was ignoring him. The

illusion would have been more effective if she had been control-
ling the eyes that were moving to keep him in view from their
corners.

"Very well, I accept the condition that you impose," he said
with a smile that almost took her breath away. "Our wager is not
for money."

The feeling came upon her that he was in some manner making
a joke with herself at the center. It was an impression she was
prepared to explore further, but an important distraction now
made itself heard.

The horses were in quick motion, and the race was being run.

Volumes have been committed to type about the proper attitude for observing a horse race when one has invested in the
outcome. In those volumes, mostly of prose but with some in
poetry so as to confuse the most ardent who wager, the virtue of
calmness is spoken of in the very highest terms. Encomiums are
offered to the practice of taking deep breaths, and at least one
commentator of note has boldly come out in favor of prayer
before and during the festivity itself. Every ritual that is cited,
even the most extreme, is intended to foster an attitude of patient
resignation to the outcome.

In the drama that we are currently observing, such rituals
would be pointless. The young woman in our charitable gaze is
anxious for her family to profit from the race, as we have seen. We
are also aware that she wishes to have a certain man proven an
inadequate prophet. As we have been attending so alertly to the
proceedings, we know, too, that she finds herself stirred by the
man's appearance and comprehending that he is not unmoved by
her. As a result, her impulses tend to dart in several directions at
the same time. That confident Cressida Fleet who is cherished by
family and friends has become, for this episode, no more than a
memory.

Patient resignation was a rare attribute for Cressida. She
watched tautly, gloved hands clenched into fists, eyes narrowed.
Even her teeth were gritted, almost as if to bite Scapegrace and
force greater speed upon him. The frenzied animal was currently
a length behind Lover's Knot, and no one could be certain that he
was going to catch up.

To do Cressida justice, she was not the only witness being made tense by the movements of half a dozen animals. Those bettors who had invested on either possible victor were behaving similarly. They seemed one and all to be shaking their heads in silently urging on whichever beast they favored. Few exceptions made themselves heard, however, good form being preserved by Sociables at all times of difficulty.

Cressida had never seen Lover's Knot run so briskly. It seemed likely that the jockey had been instructed to come out of the barrier at full power and keep the horse performing that way throughout. In such a fashion he might get and keep the jump on Scapegrace, who started full tilt and held back nothing. (It did not occur to Cressida that she and the latter horse had much in common.) If she had been instructing the jockey on handling Lover's Knot for this race, she would have been firm about the point.

Consequently it came as no surprise to see Lover's Knot virtually sail across the finish line first.

Muffled groans proceeded from the losing investors, while exultant little breaths of relief issued from the throats of their more fortunate brethren. The responses were no different than those at the end of many other races that Cressida had closely observed.

She turned slowly from the gentleman who had stood so excitingly near. As she had not been able to tell in advance which of two steeds would emerge triumphant, she felt certain that he could not be impressed with her.

Carefully she avoided her mother's eyes, which she knew would be steely with reproach. Because of looking elsewhere, she saw another gentleman come rushing in her direction. This was a frail-looking young man, blond, with watery eyes. Just as she was wincing at his closeness, he swerved from her and faced someone else.

"A good show, Jemmy," this one said loudly and clearly, though short of breath as a result of his recent gyrations. He wanted everyone in earshot to know that he was acquainted with the owner of the winning horse.

"Yes, I'm proud of Lover's Knot myself," said the owner.

Cressida started to turn back when she heard that familiar

voice. Impulsively she wanted to offer congratulations from the bottom of her heart. The victory had been earned by hard work and deserved the highest acknowledgment.

On second thought she resumed her walk to the nearest exit. Having failed as she had done, he almost certainly would not wish to endure any further traffic with her. She had been in error about more than the outcome of one race.

"Pardon me now, but I do have to arrange matters," said the young man known as Jemmy.

The friend murmured something Cressida did not hear.

No doubt Jemmy would be on his way down to the track level and the company of his winning animal. In Lover's Knot's immediate presence he would sunnily accept congratulations from a steward of the Jockey Club or some minor functionary.

She watched him in motion, back straight, head erect. Confidence brimmed in him along with each surging step he took, and he exuded pride in being young and successful. Watching him forever, or so it seemed, would have been as great a happiness as might be granted to a female.

Only when he was out of sight did she try to remember the name of the owner of Lover's Knot. In this she was having only partial success, although she had read it casually in the *Racing Intelligencer,* also in *Racing Days* and *Racing Today.* Unless an owner had brought many winners to the track in the last few years, she took no note whatever of his identity.

She had been struck in this case by the knowledge that he was a peer and that he had to train his horses as well as race them. Most of his income, therefore, was gained by the success of certain animals. He was as dependent on the prowess of various beasts as were Cressida and her family. Small wonder there had been antagonism between him and her. Given any sustained closeness, it must be that inevitable differences would grow on both sides and cause mutual antagonism.

There would have been no basis of reality in her brief fantasies about Lord Dunster. The name had been recollected while she was not giving the full weight of her intellect to that matter. Since meeting him casually it did seem that she was unable to think with her usual clarity.

Further thoughts of Lord Jeremy Dunster (from a village in

Shropshire, if she was not mistaken) were promptly relegated to consideration at a later time. This was the moment when her father and brother were making a joint appearance upon the horizon.

"I am sorry that I picked the wrong one," she said to the duo when they had joined their mother in a rough circle.

"Fortunately," Mr. Fleet responded, wiping his forehead vigorously, "there is a compensation. You took so long to make a choice that neither your brother nor I was able to reach a turf accountant in time to accept the wagers."

"You relieve my mind."

"Without cause entirely, I fear. I had informed my usual turf accountant, Passy the Prince of Payers as he is known, that I would bet on that race. When I did not do so, he felt that I must have taken my custom elsewhere and was only pretending to regrets. He was bitter. Turf accountants have their virtues, I suppose, but generosity with lines of credit is not among them. I anticipate a future difficulty along that line with Passy, and I may have to end up taking my patronage elsewhere."

Cressida made every effort to discover a bright side in opposition to this litany of minor disaster with which she had been favored. "At least you won't have to go to Tattersall's on Monday to pay for any mistaken wager."

Mama, of course, put in practically, "Or collect from a turf accountant, either."

"I cannot always guess correctly," Cressida remarked, justifying herself weakly in the face of collective gloom. "I am not blessed with occult powers."

"Spare us the sarcasm," said Hartley Fleet with an unconvincing brusqueness.

Mama, of course, had considered the setback long enough to diagnose a likely reason for it.

"Our daughter, Mr. Fleet, was busily making eyes at a young man, so she was unable to concern herself with her family's needs."

Mr. Fleet looked uncomfortable. He wanted Cressida to find a splendid suitor without any interference in the family earnings, but it was only Mama who reluctantly realized the impossibility of such a desirable outcome.

Cressida heard herself saying, "That young man is a—is a fool, a dismal fool!"

The disclaimer of interest in a male was received variously by the family. Hartley Fleet nodded in grim-lipped satisfaction. Torin looked unsettled, but sedulously avoided inspecting his sister as if to determine the veracity of her statement. Mama alone seemed entirely unconvinced, though she said nothing more in this public place. She would have been the last to deny that the subject contributed nothing to her peace of mind, but accepted that it must occasionally be discussed.

Torin glanced about him at the Sociables on the way back to their homes or to carriages or trains that would return them to London.

"We had best take to the carriage," said Cressida's brother. Certainly he had inherited Mrs. Fleet's vein of practicality if not in quite so virulent a form.

The family turned and started out, taking a northerly direction to the exit. The men walked together, with Mrs. Fleet behind them. Cressida, as a certain indicator of status lost for this day at least, was left to walk out after the others.

Rebelliously for once, she gave them considerable room. Mama looked back first from a distance. Clearly Mrs. Fleet was in sympathy with another female, but declined to break ranks and make her feelings apparent. Torin looked back and nodded gravely.

Papa took longest to meet her eyes and turned away almost immediately. Hartley Fleet had gone through much of his life thinking of himself as a worldly man devoid of fellow feeling for any who had erred, but in this assessment of himself he was mistaken.

Cressida became aware of murmurs behind her, of congratulations that were offered and accepted by a male whose voice would be familiar to her ever afterward because of this afternoon's previous events.

Lord Jeremy Dunster suddenly said, "Ah, there you are!"

Cressida turned in time to see his lordship's splendidly roughened features once more. He was smiling at her now and none other.

Her surprise gave way to astonishment. Jeremy Dunster suddenly approached. His body was in front of her and hiding Cressida from the sight of any family member who might choose to look back yet again. His arms were placed against the small of her back and his head moved as he drew it down to kiss her.

She took to this new experience with pleasure. It was difficult, though, to suppress amazement that he could show fondness for her even though she had been badly mistaken about a matter of importance.

She was on the point of returning the pressure when he suddenly raised his head. He must have become aware of rising murmurs on all sides of them.

"I had forgotten to tell you the terms of the bet we made," said his lordship, grinning. "If your nominee had won, then you would have had to kiss me!"

A young male called out, "Hoo-rah!", and she heard rising applause under which his weakened voice was clear.

"I had no plans to do that, no plans at all!"

A circle of young Sociables were taking him away from her. All of them would be celebrating his victory far into the night.

A palpable shock came to her within moments. One certain man was glancing coldly at her from over a shoulder, the pale friend who had first congratulated Jeremy Dunster upon his victory. He looked as if he had previously overheard her telling the family that Dunster was a fool, a dismal fool! Very likely he would shortly be repeating those words to Dunster.

Little wonder that Cressida was deeply upset. On this one afternoon, when she might have changed her life out of all knowledge, she felt convinced she had ruined it instead, ruined it beyond recall!

CHAPTER THREE

She was in no better a frame of mind when the family reached home in London's Albemarle Street. Nor was she in any condition to do handsprings of joy two days later when she walked into the morning room to start a day's work.

The room was perfectly comfortable. Sunlight through the opened so-called garden window, which gave a better view of Grafton Street than it did of the back-of-the-house garden, fell in such a way that she could pause in the middle of any efforts and close her eyes and soothe herself by turning towards it. The turquoise-blue wallpaper set Cressida's paleness off as few other colors did, in her opinion. Over the unused fire screen, the black mantel firmly held her recently acquired copy of *Aphrodite* in case she wanted to read a sin-steeped book of revelry in ancient times. The rocking chair was beyond praise, the Eastlake desk wide enough for her purpose, and the Iranian rug was suitable for pacing in dissatisfaction.

The rug was being used now.

Cressida had imagined that Lord Jeremy Dunster, beside filling her dreams and many of her waking moments, would be communicating with her, asking whether he had actually been called a fool. Pointedly, too, he would want to know if she was coldly indifferent to his closeness, the touch of his lips on hers.

She hadn't been indifferent.

As heaven was her witness, she hadn't been!

She had seen the prospect of happiness coming into her previously restricted life. Lord Dunster, attracted by her as well, made it clear by reaching his hands around her waist. His features, roughened pleasantly by the fresh air at race meetings, had drawn closer until she wished fervently that the two of them were anywhere but at a racetrack in Cheshire and that they were alone. His nearness would make the males in M. Pierre Louys's romance of *Aphrodite* seem like so many baked-boiled potatoes.

Instead he had drawn up to her, then pulled back, and was keeping his distance. Sulking in his tent, perhaps, so to speak.

She might have taken the next step and reached him by post. In a different situation, she would not have hesitated for a moment. But there wasn't any way of knowing whether Lord Dunster had been told what she said. If she suddenly apologized she'd have seemed like a malicious fool, further offending a man of godlike handsomeness who might not have known he had been offended in the first place.

These thoughts had been impelled upon her, as she soon realized, by a series of idle fantasies rippling across her mind's eye. Cressida drew a deep breath and forced herself to send them packing.

She was at home, in the four-story house on Albemarle Street in June of '97. This was everyday life in which her prime duty was that of earning bread and butter and an occasional scone for herself and her family. This was reality.

And at the moment, in line with her feelings during these last couple of days, Cressida Fleet hated reality.

She could hear the unmistakably youthful steps of her brother turning in from Grafton Street and reaching the house. He passed the porticoed front entrance and marched through the wide hall. He passed the dining room. There was a split-moment's pause before he knocked on the half-open door to the morning room. He marched in without waiting for her response.

Under his right arm were a handful of racing papers. The writers who contributed to them always undertook to predict the winners of various contests that involved horses in competition. To accomplish that worthy goal, as it sometimes appeared, they resorted to tea-leaf reading or crystal ball prognostication. It wasn't true, as some racecourse wit had suggested, that the journalists reached their results by reading the entrails of a turf accountant.

Cressida inspected these penny papers once a week to make note of the reasoning by which various sages arrived at opposing conclusions. One never knew what information might be useful. By the application of such a method among others in the last two years, she had been helped to get some fine results. Any fool could have picked the Prince of Wales's Persimmon to take Ascot, but it needed intelligence of a particular order to have picked well at the Oakes, the St. Leger, the Doncaster, the Caesarewich, the Hunt, the Steward's, and a few others. She'd had her failures, being no more than human in spite of her stunned father's occasional awed praises after a run of successful bets. The average of wins had been high enough, however, to cause her family to keep her occupied at pursuing horses, so to speak, rather than prospective husbands.

She started to leaf idly through the penny racing sheet at hand, hoping that she wouldn't come across the name of one special owner. Her interest wasn't as high as at the peak season, with Ascot having been run in May and Goodwood not due until July. Race meetings in between had to be attended selectively, though, and it was Cressida's task to identify those horses who might perform creditably.

She noticed, amused, that a race to be run at Herts would be populated by horses named, among others, Gwyn, Maintenon, and Chudleigh. It seemed shameful that there was no man to whom she could confide the mildly ribald thought that had crossed her mind.

There was one man, but he—never mind!

She was turning the fragile page of cheap paper when she became aware that her older brother hadn't made the first motion to leave. In a grave manner his bright blue eyes inspected her.

"I've been thinking, Cressy. The people who buy these penny papers every day, those people spend coppers they can't afford."

"It's better for them than buying gin. Or listening to maundering brothers." She was too distracted to think about good manners. "Is there a point to all this, or are you planning a disquisition about the virtues of reading?"

"I have been thinking that it would be profitable to own a penny paper of this type."

"And it would be profitable to own the Crystal Palace as well."

"I am serious, Cressy. If we owned a racing paper, no one in the family would have to travel any longer, except for pleasure."

"Mama and Papa are fond of that activity, and no matter what the state of their income they would be like migratory birds."

"And you, Cressy, you could stop doing this work of yours and involve yourself with the womanly activity of seeking a husband."

Torin must have felt that he in turn could then address himself to the task of finding a suitable wife and fathering a suitable dynasty. As the bringer-in of family moneys, he'd no longer have to depend for his sole income on work done by a mere female. He had thought of other schemes to achieve those same ends in the past, but every one of them was cursed by the same drawback.

"What you say, Torin, might be true, but the possibility of it happening is nil, as it has been with other ideas of yours. The family exchequer isn't of such a magnitude as to allow for the sort of purchase you have in mind."

Torin writhed like an eel. It couldn't have been any pleasure to be told the plain truth by a three-years-younger sister who ought to have been going to dances or balls and giggling with girl-friends about the behavior of certain young males. Or better yet, as he had more than hinted, who should have spent one day's canonical hours from eight to three in the task of getting married.

"With a line of credit," he persisted, "we could found a racing paper of our own."

"And who is such a dunce as to give credit to a family—"

"A family that remains part of society," he reminded her, "as it was before falling on hard times."

"—a family, as I was in the act of saying, whose only income is derived from one member's assessment of the improving of the breed."

Torin, blessed by the variety of bulldog pluck that had won through at Waterloo, wasn't giving up easily.

"We would only have to put half the money up if I could find an owner who wants to take in a partner."

"You would still have to be able to call upon a line of credit in case of need." Cressida shrugged regretfully, the azure cashmere day dress moving discreetly with her shoulders. "If you can per-suade Papa and Mama to the merit of your proposal, we would all talk it over *en famille* and determine what might be made of it. But

I fancy you would be wasting your efforts as they will surely have none of it."

"You're right," Torin admitted miserably. "I've tried more than once. Papa says bluntly that my notion is impractical. Mama dislikes the uncertainty of our income's source in the behavior of horses, so she would be fertile ground, you would think, for my scheme. Not at all. She said that what I want might indeed be done if certain conditions were met, but gave so many conditions as to make the entire project unfeasible. You know the way Mama can be."

Cressida did indeed. Mama was fully capable of considering a course of action in such a way as to make it clear that it would only be adopted over the impediment of her dead body. It was a trait that Cressida disliked. More than once she had told herself that when she was Mama's age and full of years and honor, she would remain as forthright—not to say on occasion as tactless—as she was now.

"If you could only see it my way," Torin said, unwilling to leave the morning room in spite of his sister's pointed silence. "I'm sure that Mama and Papa would come around."

He was half right. This time. Papa, awed by his daughter's skill at predicting the outcome of many races, had become a shade more respectful than a father ought to be if he wants her to admire him. Mama, of course, always managed to have things done pretty much the way she thought was best for all the members of her family.

"Very well," Torin said at this latest and longest silence. "I confess that I've been too farsighted, too daring for my family to accept what I say. From now on I will be a member in good standing who does what he is told and nothing more."

Cressida looked up for the first time in minutes. It was on the tip of her tongue to tell him how much she sympathized with his desire to earn the family income and with his clear but unstated longing for a wife as well.

Her sympathies were not to be expressed this time. The morning room door flew open on Mama, who entered and noticed the racing papers on Cressida's Eastlake desk.

"I have something to take up with you, Cressy," she said firmly.

Papa, having come in with diffidence behind his wife, also noticed the racing papers.

"Cressy, I, too, have something to discuss with you," he said. "If you'll give your permission, of course."

CHAPTER FOUR

Papa planted his feet apart and began to speak further while Torin was being directed by Mama to leave the morning room without standing on ceremony.

"You are surely aware, Cressy, that my father, your paternal grandfather, earned a fortune by his many investments in the stock market," he proceeded, as if reading aloud from a paper about some scientific discovery.

"Yes, of course, Papa."

"You realize, then, that he had a certain instinct, a certain flair, as you yourself do with the horses."

Cressida was at a loss to make out the importance of such a reminder. A cloud passed over Papa's normally smooth features. Not for the first time he must have been regretting the lack of any such instinct in himself.

"One can only regret that the money was—ah—diminished by the passage of time," Papa muttered, more to himself than his daughter.

Cressida didn't point out that the passage of time must have been aided by Papa's trying to equal Sir Whitman Fleet's achievement by making investments of his own. There had been an important difference between the efforts of father and son, however, the latter's investments going down in value like the sun in the evening.

Mama, turning away from Torin's departing figure, had taken note of what was happening. Rather than interrupt, perhaps bruising her husband's feelings as a result, she waited tactfully for the matter to be concluded.

"Among other firms that repaid your grandfather's confidence a thousandfold, Cressy, was an enterprise named Flagitious—ah, Enterprises, I believe. I am not entirely certain of what the firm's efforts consisted of. I remember having heard, though, that they imported tea from one of Bulldom's Oriental possessions and resold it to the same country at an enormous profit. That doesn't sound right, somehow, but it hardly matters at the moment."

"If you say so, Papa."

He was startled by the sign of respect from a person with the exalted gift of money earning. "At any rate, Cressy, the point is— well, I won't delay you any longer. I happened to see in one of last week's racing papers, after you had finished with it, that a two-year-old who will be running next week at some course in Herts, I believe, is named Flagitious. I had it in mind to speak with you about that happy accident."

"Quite a coincidence," she said, not knowing what else to say, let alone realizing the point of the anecdote.

"I think of it as an indication."

Now she understood. "So you feel that it is a manifestation to us that we should bet on the animal."

"Certainly."

It was the last issue on earth that Cressida wanted to take up, but she hesitated no longer. Reaching for a copy of *Racing Today* and another of *Racing Time*, she found mention of the horse and conflicting reports on its ancestry and habits. *Racing Habit* was no more helpful. One striking similarity did appear in each account of the horse's few previous triumphs. She found herself reading more slowly as time passed in order to confirm the feeling that she had formed about the particular animal.

"You wouldn't favor him," Papa said after a detailed study of his daughter's facial contortions.

"Flagitious is a two-year-old who has won no more than seven races out of thirty-five starts, and those seven came early in his career," Cressida said gently. "He could certainly win at Herts, depending upon the quality of the field against him."

"But you wouldn't favor him, Cressy. I can tell that much."

"He needs prodding, Papa. He won all his races in last-minute spurts, having been held back by his riders until then. Different riders have used the whip against him, and as he's lost so often they may well have used it heavily. The sustained flogging could have hurt the animal in some way, or angered him so that he refuses to do his duty when the whip is applied. In sum, Papa, I think that Flagitious is more unreliable than a horse should be if he is to draw our custom."

"I see." Crestfallen, he turned away to join his son on the other side of the door.

"Please stay, Mr. Fleet," Mama said, and turned to their daughter. "This is a matter that involves us all, and would call for Torin's opinion as well, but he seems occupied by some other problem."

Gladys Fleet adjusted the crinkled silk doucet dress by pulling back her shoulders and drawing them toward herself. It was an unfortunate weakness of the garment that it tended to droop very slightly. Gladys Fleet was ready to adjust it when necessary so that she might wear the clothing she wanted at the price she craved. She was a woman who made her choices and was ready to live with them.

As a maiden, she had chosen Hartley Fleet for her husband, impressed by his skill at spending money. She hadn't known that he was not blessed with the capacity to replace what was gone, and once his inheritance had been spent he had no further resources. Employment, which was offered by a family friend, seemed to him at first like a fate worse than poverty. By the time he was ready to accept, the generous offer had been withdrawn, and none others were made.

The bride had seen to it that her own family came to their aid. Less money was spent by Hartley, too, and his only luxuries were newspapers and tobacco. When it turned out that their daughter had inherited Sir Whitman's gift for acquiring money in the same general way that ancient explorers had divined the presence of water on what looked like dry land, Gladys Fleet had at last begun living less modestly.

And now, or so it seemed to her, the entire system by which her family had flourished these last two years was in peril. Gladys Fleet, however, was going to do her best to keep the family solvent.

"It is a good time to discuss a family matter," she began, taking her text for the sermon. "The best time to talk about what took place at Cheshire."

Cressida, although she had become alert for a quarrel, hardly kept from sighing. What had happened was that she had seen a man who thrilled her by his handsomeness and bearing and presence, and most of all by his closeness when he had impudently kissed her. Small wonder she felt certain that her whole life had changed!

"I saw you in close conversation with a groom," Mama continued.

"He was not a groom, Mama!"

"He was dressed like a laborer, so that there is even less excuse for him if he is not a minor functionary at the racecourse."

This was not the time to put in that the young man was an owner and a peer as well. The information would have given Mama cause to suspect that her daughter had developed an increasing tendency to look away from the shopping expeditions and the racing papers that had filled almost all of Cressida's recent life.

"I hoped that he could give me some hint about the possible behavior of one of the horses."

"This was near the end of the racing day, Cressy. Don't think I've forgotten that much."

"I had to thank him for the help that he had previously given me."

"You spoke to this groom without letting any of us know," Mama pointed out, narrowing those bright blue eyes, which Cressida had inherited. "Papa or Torin would have been happy to save you the added exertion."

"I was not entirely aware what I wanted to say, Mama, until I had begun speaking to him."

There was a glint of truth in that statement, although not nearly as much as Mama may have supposed. Nevertheless it was accepted with a nod and the beginnings of a smile. Mama may have felt that if the probing went on too much longer she herself might be faced with the sort of difficulty that had confronted Captain Bligh on the ill-fated HMS *Bounty*.

"You do understand, Cressy, that Papa and I are anxious only to make your life a little easier."

"Of course."

"Should you have any similar wish, you have only to discuss it with someone, and Papa or your brother will join you for such inquiries as you feel it is necessary to make."

Cressida asked directly, "Is it so troubling if I talk to a male?"

"There is the aspect of how that sort of behavior is seen by society, daughter. Talking in confidence to a man of lower station is simply not, as I need hardly point out, done by anyone of position."

She hated to give in after keeping so much of the truth to herself, and wished she had been more in the mood for a long discussion. In that case, she would started by saying directly that the young man at Cheshire was none other than Lord Dunster, who owned a stable of horses. Saying it now would open her to another accusation of having been secretive. Under the circumstances and through no real fault of her own, there would have been some merit in the charge this time.

It made sense to keep this conversation from continuing. She, too, dreaded the possible onset of domestic turbulence.

"I will be more careful in the future, Mama." She meant every word.

"See to it that you are." Mama didn't sound as if she had been taken in by filial meekness. "I don't want you to think that Papa and I are unwilling to see you have any social congress with a male, but it has to be done in a suitable form and with males whose station in society is appropriate."

"I understand that now."

Mama was not willing to give up the podium. "After all, you are a young woman of seventeen summers and not unattractive, not at all. I could wish that you chose not to wear your hair with a topknot so that it looks like a daffodil in a wheat field, but this is a matter of personal taste and I do not venture to dictate my own preferences as long as your appearance is in an accepted mode."

"Yes, Mama."

"Further, it is possible that you might one day wish to be something other than a spinster. It would be perfectly understandable to me."

"I'm sure it would, Mama."

"Indeed, I feel that you should marry just as soon as the family can afford to lose you."

Cressida's head went down as if she was going to charge at the finish line. It took all her effort to keep from asking on what day and at what hour she would be free to begin seeking a husband.

"Be patient a little longer," Mama said.

Clearly, those words were recognized as meaningless. The older woman who felt trapped reached down a palm encouragingly to the shoulder of the younger woman who was actually trapped. Cressida was being asked for compassion, for forgiveness.

It was a clear reminder of what had happened any number of times between Mama and others in the immediate family. There would be a bone of contention, and Mama would be patient and understanding about the nature of the difficulty and the reason for somebody else's justified feelings. But it didn't happen very often as a result that any change whatever took place.

She didn't see the racing papers although they were in front of her. What she saw instead was Jeremy's strong features roughened by time spent outdoors, and the light gray eyes that warmed excitingly. What she heard was that strong and deep and pleasant voice of his. Image and sound remained clear even though he was far away.

A noise distracted her. The morning room door was being closed—firmly, so that she could work in peace and quiet.

Now she reached avidly for *Racing Days*, which was the penny paper nearest at hand. A brisk look at a list of stables and the locations of the owners' next efforts offered an excellent source of information. She was nodding firmly when she put down the paper.

Jeremy would be racing over the weekend at Foxbridge in Kent.

Her immediate dilemma was resolved. The contests had to be analyzed first. After that she would instruct her family that it was to Kent that they would all be proceeding.

She couldn't, of course, tell her reason for that unlikely choice. For her, indeed, keeping her own counsel would be the most difficult task of all.

CHAPTER FIVE

She was feeling dissatisfied at the end of two hours when she pulled away from the desk. The outcome of various races at Kent would be difficult to predict with any confidence at this stage. Some horses became mildly dizzy when confronted by a one-mile course with two turns and not even a half-chute for variety's sake. Worse yet, the directors of that course's proceedings were in the habit of ordering the turf watered between races, which seemed like a certain indicator of accidents happening to one or more of the contenders.

Speculatively, Cressida had drawn up a list of half a dozen horses whose energies might pay off to some fortunate bettors over the weekend. Those choices could be altered at the last minutes, as nearly always happened with her. A list was comforting in itself. She felt that it gave some basis for comparison.

There was an incentive for her to go off elsewhere for the balance of this afternoon. Two notes had been delivered to her on Monday morning. One was signed by Letitia Waghorn, a friend, writing that it would be pleasant to welcome Cressida at three o'clock Tuesday afternoon. The other, signed by Amaryllis Wyse, a closer friend, conveyed pleasure that they would be meeting shortly at the home of Letitia's parents.

She spoke to Mama, who happened to be knitting, and promised to return before supper. Up in her room, the sunniest in the house and perhaps in all Albemarle Street, she put on a travelling cloak. Its lustrous *drap de soie* surface made it clear to any distant male eye that a young woman was in the offing. The stiff-brimmed straw hat with loops and flower clusters was enough to confirm the initial impression. The large ruche of tosca net around the neck was her favorite accessory because it gave her an air of mystery. Any acquaintance would have agreed that mystery was entirely at odds with her character.

Mama had insisted that she take the four-in-hand, probably so that Daymore, the coachman, would be able to report afterward on the subject of Cressida's whereabouts. Seen through the window, London was sunny if not as warm as might be expected for this time of year. It almost seemed as if a day in April would be as rare as this day in June. But the trip passed pleasantly enough, except for a moment when the sound of a locomotive surging out of Victoria Station convinced the horses that the world had suddenly come to an end.

She sensed something amiss soon after she rang the visitors' bell in the Grosvenor Street home and the dark-painted door wasn't opened immediately. When it did open, the fiftyish butler stood in the doorway brushing his gray-tinged chin whiskers with a thumbnail rather than courteously standing aside. The footsteps of a young woman hurried down the hall toward her.

"I'm so glad you came at last," said Amaryllis Wyse as the butler belatedly stood aside. "Letitia has begun feeling indisposed, but has sent a message asking us to wait for her recovery if it takes no more than half the hour."

Amaryllis embraced her in a gingerly way, careful to preserve the folds of her dress. A practical girl, the dark-haired and wide-eyed Amaryllis put in much of her time at the fine art of husband hunting. No male who had crossed her path as of this date and was eligible for matrimony had met her basic requirement of above-average wealth. Mama had once guessed that Amaryllis would probably spend three more years in the hunt for financial perfection, then give up the quest and marry the next merely wealthy man who showed interest in her.

The drawing room, which both girls entered, bulged with masses of dark furniture. No one else was in the room.

"I suppose that Letitia's papa and mama are with her at this difficult time," Cressida said. A soft groan had drifted down from the drawing room landing.

"Her papa is at work in his railroad building enterprise, and her mama has left to plan a charity event for the ill," Amaryllis said briskly.

Another groan from above was curdled into a thin wail before subsiding. The housekeeper, hearing it, moved more quickly down the hallway with its scrawny lamps and outsize mirrors that caused everybody looking into them to resemble her own ghost. She was escorting a bearded and important-looking man with a black bag. This medical practitioner would care for Letitia at a sizable fee.

"I have much gossip to tell you," said Amaryllis, who had noted the new arrival and probably identified the amount of his savings. "You know Cyril Eviot, of course. Cyril has been drinking so much, my dear, that no female in her right mind would consider him as a mate, even if his family was possessed of more money than it is."

Amaryllis stopped briefly, asking herself whether she would marry a wine-bibber if he was wealthy. Leaving the question unresolved in her mind, as it would have needed much thought, she moved to another item.

"Eunice Boley is finally wed to Ivor Satterthwaite. Not a surprise, as they've known each other from childhood. They were given a huge ceremony at St. George's in Hanover Square. The best was what Eunice deserved, being ultrarespectable, as Ivor himself has always been."

"There's more to this story," Cressida said perceptively as her friend paused.

"Quite right, Cress. A condition was laid down by Mrs. Boley or the Satterthwaites or both. It was simply that Eunice and Ivor take the dowry and move out to Australia, never to return to this shore. Isn't that simply smashing?"

"Too much respectability from a young person is wearing, but from a young male and female in tandem it can be stupefying," Cressida remarked. "I always felt, when in the company of one or the other or both, as if I had just dropped an entire tea seat on the foot of some old gentleman with the gout."

A more pleasant item of news remained to be passed on. "Would you believe that Cyril Maudsley—that frightful infant who once swallowed a whole set of illustrated *Tales from the Holy Land* on cards—is now attending Harrow and will be at Balliol before either of us knows it? My dear, if there was enough money in the family I would seriously consider despoiling the cradle and sneaking off with him to Gretna Green."

"The girl he will eventually marry is probably now at that point in life when she is learning to put one foot in front of the other."

"Ah, I fear so!" Amaryllis could appreciate the grim side to the news of Cyril Maudsley's increasing maturity. "Time and tide wait for no one, as the saying is—approximately. It behooves us, Cress, not only to make plans for the future but to carry them out."

An idea had come to Cressida as she listened. Impelled by her friend's now looking favorably upon the thought of stirring one's self to make changes, she acted on it immediately.

"Amaryllis, you spend far more time in London than I do, so—"

"Only because I am not perpetually off to the racing," Amaryllis interrupted, with a show of rectitude that would have impressed Eunice and Ivor Satterthwaite. "There is a time for racing and a time for husband hunting, and the two are often in conflict."

"I was about to say that you are acquainted with more young men than I am."

"If a man is young, eligible, and a Sociable as well, I know him. If he is rich, I can tell more about him than anyone except his solicitor."

"Do you know Jeremy Dunster?"

"Lord Jemmy? But of course." Amaryllis's eyes now seemed even wider than nature had intended. "He races the horses he owns and trains them as well, and you and your family are great followers of the track. It is incomprehensible to me that you would not know Jemmy."

"I know him hardly at all."

Amaryllis sat down suddenly in the walnut chair opposite, smoothing her turquoise day dress and its stitched satin bands. She was preparing for an intimate conversation. "Well, my dear, you must know that he does not suffer from a surfeit of the necessary. He could hardly support a wife in anything that resembled a proper style."

"How unfortunate," Cressida murmured.

"I understand, too, that the mama of many an anxious miss has mistaken him for a mere groom or a stable lad at the races."

"My mama did so, too," Cressida admitted.

"Many a mother finds his behavior unseemly, being distressed that he should concern himself so with the welfare of animals. Rather than spending day in and day out with the infernal beasts, sportsmen should simply see to it that the menials perform their assigned tasks, and confine his own efforts to accepting the awards that are offered for victories on the turf."

"Perhaps." Cressida had never given the least thought to her feelings if she ever met a peer who chose to train his own horses.

"My advice in this matter of the heart has not been requested, Cress, but as I am not wholly without experience in these situations I venture to offer it all the same."

"And it is?"

"Give Jemmy Dunster a wide berth."

"Might I ask why you feel so strongly that I should have nothing to do with Lord Dunster?"

"Oh, it's not because of Jemmy himself, you great goose! Jemmy is a fine fellow, handsome and thoughtful and even rather intelligent as the run of sportsmen go, in my limited experience. It's entirely a matter of what it is that he represents."

"And what would that be?"

"His racing, my dear," Amaryllis said, as if she was using the sort of logic that ought to have been plain to the youngest and dimmest. "There can be no assurance that he will turn away from his steeds long enough to marry you or any female."

"You mean that he is excessively occupied with training and racing horses?"

"In part, Cress, I do. But I also mean that you should no longer give over nearly so much time to attending race meetings at all."

"I beg your pardon?" Cressida would have sworn that she had been listening alertly to her friend's every word, but none of them when put together made the least sense.

"You have spent excessive amounts of time at the racing course and among men who are older or relatively impoverished. Instead, you should be involved in the pursuit of a husband worthy of you."

It was impossible for the direct and normally truthful Cressida to give the facts about her family's source of income. To ensure her own silence at this juncture, she bit down so forcefully on her lower lip that she almost cried out.

Amaryllis must have thought that the silence was caused by confusion and guilt. She resumed with fresh energy.

"You have been led into this error because of the habits of the elders in your family, I don't doubt. Many of our friends don't doubt that, either."

"You've talked about this with friends of ours?"

"Certainly I have, and we are all concerned for you. We feel sure that you at least are on the point of becoming a slave to wagering in the same way that an opium fiend is held in thrall by opium."

Cressida said quietly, as much to herself as to her friend, "I do not believe I am hearing this."

"Certainly you feel that you can withdraw at any time you wish, but gambling is not that sort of pursuit, Cress. Your other friends and I, all of us ask you to give thought to your future. You must shake off this foul habit while you still can, *if* you still can, this obsession that has kept you from searching out a husband worthy of you."

Cressida told herself that all her friends meant well. Their arguments were entirely sensible. Against them there was only the single particular drawback, which couldn't be mentioned but effectively canceled every point that had been raised.

An interruption was welcome as it kept her from saying what was on her mind. The housekeeper, who had crossed the girls' field of vision a while ago, was entering the morning room and clearing her throat softly but persistently as she moved.

"Please excuse me, *mesdemoiselles.*"

She sounded like one of those French performers on a revue stage, but the black dress identified her as a staff member. Her smile managed to be solemn and ingratiating at the same time.

"I regret to say as Mademoiselle Letitia will not be well today."

Amaryllis nodded. "Please give Miss Letitia our wishes for a speedy recovery."

"Indeed yes," said Cressida. Brief and informal though her assent might have been, it was the more heartfelt expression of sympathy.

"Mademoiselle Letitia also asks me to post you that she will see you both tomorrow night."

Cressida assumed that the Toast of Paree had made more than

one mistake in transmitting the message. Amaryllis, however, took it in stride.

Cressida courteously walked behind her friend on the way to the outer door, pausing to retrieve the traveling cloak that she had shed upon arrival.

Amaryllis halted thoughtfully in front of the iron gate on the street. "I doubt if the prestige of having a French housekeeper is worth having to listen to her struggles with the mother tongue."

"I had no idea what she meant about Letitia seeing us tomorrow night."

"But I was sure you knew about that, Cress. I do believe I mentioned it briefly a few moments ago."

"You mentioned it to me?"

"Briefly, my dear, a ball is to be held at the Waghorn home tomorrow night for a charity that aids those who are ill. Letitia's mama is on the committee in charge, and Letitia, health permitting, will of course be in attendance and eagle-eyed for a potential suitor. As will we all."

"I had no idea of this."

"You have been too busy at other pursuits to aid the ill. But I speak no more of that. I do think that tickets for you and your family can still be obtained."

"I will discuss it with them."

She wasn't inclined to make an appearance. She'd be unhappy all night long if Amaryllis and some of their mutual friends spent time talking about her nonexistent addiction. It would be a deplorable few hours if she attended.

"In the meantime, Cress, you might care to do some shopping with me. I don't mean buying, of course, which requires parental permission."

Let Cressida refuse, and it would seem as if the recent talk had made her angry. She found herself, on consideration, feeling touched that a friend would show enough concern to bring up a point that was so thorny.

"Let us indeed shop, sister," Cressida smiled. "I have a carriage at the curb."

"That will be excellent," Amaryllis agreed.

CHAPTER SIX

In her close-fitting basque dress, with silk collar and cuffs and fashionable silk pockets at the back, Mama looked contented. The family was gathering in front of the dining room and waiting for supper to be announced.

Cressida, in a black worsted polka-dot dress that showed off her light hair, stepped back to give Mama a more balanced view of narrow flounces shirred and pleated, of drapery shortened to show a satin striped skirt.

Mama said judiciously, "Your choice is by no means a bad one if you insist upon following the current inclination to buy clothes that have already been run up. But I do wish I had been present to help you with the final choice."

Cressida cast her eyes down at this gentle rebuke. Amaryllis had also been unsettled by the bold gesture of making a purchase without a mother to guide her.

"I must admit that the current styles favor youth," Mama added. "Probably they always should."

"Youth and middle age, both," Cressida responded tactfully.

Mama smiled in appreciation, but only briefly.

"I would have expected you to order a rig suitable for tomorrow night's charity function at Dorothy Waghorn's home, Cressy dear. You certainly can't wear that to a ball."

It seemed as if all London but she had been notified about the forthcoming function!

"I am not sure I will attend."

"That is your decision to make, of course," Mama said, not quarreling frivolously with that one person who was provider of the family fortunes.

Torin was speaking to his father about the business of issuing periodicals. Since the idea had first come to him, he had made a number of inquiries. He already sounded as experienced as if he had been a dealer in news printed on stone tablets during biblical times.

". . . get that paper out. Mr. Bellew is convinced that with so advanced a method a paper could be on sale at Wimbledon, for example, long before . . ."

The housekeeper, Mrs. Durbin, opened the closed double door and announced quietly but pointedly that supper was ready.

Mama allowed Torin to take her hand as they led the others into the large room with its triptych screen that could be drawn to one side in winter to show the fireplace. Table and chairs were covered in velvet, and frill-shaded lamps illuminated the lace-covered sideboard on which they rested. Mama considered the room to be comfortable and without a superfluous inch of decoration.

Over the clear soup with which the meal began, Papa addressed himself in answer to his son.

"Facts should be faced, Torin. Uncertainty is a bad companion and it is best to anticipate the worst conditions by which we may be confronted."

"You mean that there isn't money enough in the family to give me a start toward earning for myself."

Cressida, feeling sorry for him, asked, "Can nothing be done to raise the money?"

"I assure you, Cressy, that your papa and I have given some thought to this matter," said Mama reluctantly. "In spite of your best efforts there are only sufficient available funds to let us keep up with these bare necessitities of life."

She gestured around the room as broiled *capons à l'éscarlate* were being brought in on covered silver trays, illustrating the bare necessities of life to her satisfaction and probably to Papa's.

Cressida couldn't bring herself to look in sympathy at her brother's inflamed features. She looked down instead. Remembering a game that the two of them had played in childhood, she inspected her image in the teacup and then touched it lightly with the rounded end of her spoon to see the image blur.

Not for the first time, Mama made a practical suggestion. "Torin, it has been pointed out before that you should consider the use of a wife's dowry, which could be yours only after marriage."

"Marriage," Torin said flatly.

"It is a satisfactory experience," Papa put in, speaking far more autocratically to the nonearning Torin than he ever would have done to Cressida. "Every man should marry in spite of possible—ah, difficulties, which are certainly of no real importance."

"I'm not sure of that. A woman in your life in the morning and at night may not understand your feelings and woes."

Cressida was sure that her brother was justifying a course that he had unwillingly decided to adapt. Certainly he wanted to marry, but not for a father-in-law's money. Males could indulge themselves in such scruples.

"One last resort that occurs to me is at least better than living from a female's bounty," Torin said, picking at the meringue topping of the Charlotte russe, which had been put before him. "I refer to my entering the army or, at the very worst, the navy."

"Only if we could afford to buy a commission for you, Torin, would there be that choice," Mama put in. "But as Papa will inform you we cannot spare the money and hope to survive as we are."

Torin looked sharply at his mother. It was impossible not to guess at the thought crossing his mind: In no sphere of life would he ever be of any account.

"I am sorry that you are disgruntled by my thinking of myself as a person with wishes and feelings of my own," he said finally.

Papa snapped, "What's needed is a person with understanding."

Torin remained silent under the brief onslaught. When it was over his lips parted.

"May I be excused, guv'nor?" he asked, having correctly placed a napkin at the side of his teacup. He was trying to show himself as calm and unflurried.

"I suppose—why, yes," Papa agreed, but only after looking at his wife.

Now that no more than three family members remained in the dining room, Mama apparently decided that the subject of conversation would only be changed for the better. There was some discussion of the Kent races, but it didn't last long. Cressida's elders weren't prepared to question their daughter's judgment in matters of racing.

After a brief but irritable look at her husband, Mama accepted the responsibility of intruding on the pause that followed.

"Just before supper, Cressy, you and I were talking about Dorothy Waghorn's ball. You do have a suitable gown if you decide to attend with us. The pale yellow with ruffled sleeves would do, being fashionable, although I have always maintained that ruffles make a girl look portly."

"Yes, Mama."

"And I do feel that we should attend so important a function together, all of us. Sociables will be present. As the House of Lords is in meeting this month, we can each speak separately to many horse owners and glean information that may be of financial value to us."

"Yes, that is true, of course."

Her interest had been stirred, but for reasons that could not have been anticipated by a fractious parent. With the conditions that Mama had described, it seemed more than likely that the ball would be attended by one certain peer. At the prospect of seeing him again, Cressida felt her heart beating furiously.

"I hope I may be permitted to change my mind and accompany you all."

Papa was self-satisfied. "I knew you would see where your duty lay."

Cressida didn't acknowledge the remark, which had no basis in fact at this time. Too late she wondered if her stillness was being silently questioned by Mama, or worse yet was being correctly interpreted.

In a flurry of activity, Cressida set down her own napkin and asked quickly whether she might be excused. She was leaving before Papa could grant permission.

As soon as she was alone in her bedroom, she inspected the pale yellow gown and then imagined dancing with the strong leader who Jeremy Dunster must be, his hands light but firm upon her, his lips soon meeting hers and bringing exquisite pressure.

She had no reason to think that she would get any sleep on this night, or that she would want to.

CHAPTER SEVEN

Torin's views about marriage, as recently expressed over the supper table to his family, had been surprising even to him. On reflection he realized that they had been formed last year at about this time, though, and his family had indirectly helped to form them. . . .

"When you spoke about a surprise for me not too long ago, guv'nor," Torin said, looking around him in awe, "you meant it in a way that I could not have anticipated."

"We hope that you will use this voyage to discover some career you can spend your life in pursuing," Papa said formally, "with the initial help your family can afford to give."

No one mentioned that it was Torin's sixteen-year-old sister's work that was making this luxury a reality for him. He did smile at Cressida, though, thanking her without words.

It was the guv'nor who led the way proudly to the main deck of the Brevard Company's *Strength of Britain* and past rows of passenger luggage into the first stateroom amidships. The saltbox-sized chamber would be Torin's home for his six-week trip to New York City.

There was a foghorn noise, and Mr. Brevard's steamship was preparing to leave. The captain must have finally been satisfied that enough water had been taken aboard.

One of Torin's early thoughts about this trip had been that he would prefer a holiday at Margate or Brighton-by-the-sea. He wasn't going to America for a holiday, however. The reason for his visit was grim and earnest, involving as it did the remaining years of his life.

He wouldn't have felt shaky at Brighton, though. With much

difficulty, caused by the ship's being in motion under his feet, he staggered into his cabin for the first night in mid-ocean. He nearly fell while snuffing out the overhead light before getting into bed for a night's forgetfulness. His attempt at sleep came to very little. Not far off he could hear the soft moo of the ship's cow, and it kept up at intervals until morning.

Torin remained immured in his cabin for two days.

When he came to the surface at last, his sharp eyes soon observed that many other passengers had elected to stay below. He felt almost as if he had much of the ship to himself. He and the captain were often the only diners at the baize-cloth-covered captain's table.

"So many people are seasick, but all that they ever seem to talk about when they do come up is food and more food. Why is that, sir?"

"Young man, I have occasionally considered that riddle myself," said Captain Birchwood amiably. "I suggest the guinea fowl tonight, followed by apples with rice and Darjeeling tea."

Torin was starting to think favorably about the occupation of ship's captain, a man with control over every aspect of his working life. It seemed the sort of existence he could accept and even come to relish.

His mind was changed one night after he had been sitting alone and watching the ocean's water, bluer now that the ship wasn't near land. Some activity could be heard behind him and he turned. In the saloon a steward had started to drop curtains on the upholstered benches pushed back against three walls. He was providing accommodation for those passengers in the so-called tourist class.

Torin watched long enough for an idea to form in his mind. Eagerly he approached Captain Birchwood, who had been on the way to the ship's engine room.

"It occurred to me, Captain, that the travel time of first-class passengers would pass more pleasantly if the saloon could be kept open all night."

Captain Birchwood smiled. "What d'ye propose, my good young sir, that we do with the tourist class passengers? It's difficult enough to send them off in the daytime."

"Assign them permanently to another part of the ship."

"Space is at a premium on an oceangoing vessel. Even if that objection could be met, and (mind!) it couldn't, having a change adopted by the firm is not easy."

Torin was dismayed to have been suddenly proved wrong in the assumption about the independence of a sea dog of Birchwood's rank. A captain ruled only at the pleasure of his ship's owners, it now appeared. If their whims were those of arrogant men, a captain became no more than another employee.

"If you'll excuse me now, young sir—"

"Yes, of course, Captain Birchwood. Gladly."

A party was being given by the captain. First-class passengers appeared shakily in the saloon during the early evening before the *Strength of Britain* was due to dock at New York's South Street Seaport. They tried to be cheery after protracted bouts of seasickness, but their pasty faces conveyed a pronounced lack of ease. Torin felt like he was in a large but cozy room with so many animated *blancs manges*.

He started to the door almost as soon as six musicians took up their instruments. Along the way, he became aware of a young woman sitting with her parents. The young woman smiled at him. He returned the smile and walked outside to get back to staring moodily at the Atlantic Ocean.

The young woman, walking insecurely because of the ship's motions, appeared at the railing near him. She looked fragile, a small-boned miss with dark hair. The cashmere shawl around her neck and the thick dress in five colors weren't enough to keep her from shivering lightly.

"Isn't it a shame that we're taking the saloon so the tourist-class passengers can't go to sleep early if they want to? The poor people don't get to have much of anything, I don't suppose."

"You must be American," Torin said, smiling as he got to his feet. "How do you do? I am Torin Fleet."

"Annie Carr here. Glad to meet you."

He had a feeling that Miss Carr was going to extend a hand for him to clasp and waggle up and down, Yankee style. She refrained. She wasn't the only one in her family with some regard for tradition. The girl's mother was standing in front of the exit door from the saloon, not so far away that she couldn't see or so near that she could hear her daughter and a young man in conversation.

Miss Carr lived in New York City with her parents, as she didn't hesitate to say before any question along that line might have been asked. The Carrs had been to Europe visiting relatives of her mother's, who hailed from a burg called Dee-john. In France.

Torin volunteered very little about himself in exchange, only that he was meeting an uncle and hoped he'd do some traveling in the States.

"You have to look me up while you're in New York," Annie Carr said, and gave a home address on Fourth Avenue in the Twenties.

Torin responded politely, but without eagerness. He was put off because he had seen Annie Carr's smile on the faces of dozens of young females with marriage in mind. Marriage, at this time, was far from his own mind.

Miss Carr suddenly seemed to push herself toward him, and for a moment he had the horrific thought that she was literally going to be tossed at his head. A part of his mind was aware that the ship had negotiated a series of ocean waves with even less than its usual smoothness, affecting Annie Carr more than himself. He caught her extended hands in his.

Turning, he saw that the girl's mother had advanced on them. Mrs. Carr scooped up Annie without a word to him or the girl and started leading her below decks, no doubt to the family refuge.

The balance of the night passed peacefully for him.

The City of New York, seen by morning light, looked like a shabbier version of London. The traffic reminded Torin of the worst of Cheapside. The clothes worn by passersby were cut more roughly than in London. The Metropolitan Hotel, at which his uncle registered him, had been decorated by some mad horticulturist spreading dead flowers and sickly plants throughout.

Torin's first supper in America was no bargain for quality. Over a gilt tablecloth at Delmonico's Restaurant, he and Uncle Ferdy ate cold soup, a paltry remove, cold fish, which would have been far better prepared at home, and a dessert that looked like hokey-pokey but tasted more like curdled milk. His tea was too weak, and the gin and hot water much too strong. He seemed to have made up his mind not to enjoy anything in this large country.

"And what now, young-fellow-my-lad?" Uncle Ferdy asked. He was a crabbed-looking man in his forties. "What's your next step in life, so to speak?"

"Why, to find some work that I can do and which will be profitable."

"The field is wide." Uncle Ferdy gestured with large but soft hand. "Medicine, law, the armed forces."

"The guv'nor won't see that I'm supported till I can support myself."

"You can't entirely blame him," Uncle Ferdy said, like a hanging judge adjusting the black cap. "When you were younger and could've gone to the University, you weren't inclined that way."

Torin had seen no reason at that time for submitting himself to any discipline. He winced at the memory of Torin Fleet at seventeen and eighteen.

"And now you have to find a source of income in a hurry," Ferdy Castle nodded. He had already asked after his niece and sister, as well as his brother-in-law. "You might save time and effort for yourself, and marry a young woman who has got buckets of the needful."

That was a suggestion that Mama had made on several occasions. He was often pointing out by way of rebuttal that a rich marriage was no substitute whatever for work, for a career.

"Well, I suppose you could start by coming down to my office tomorrow morning and looking around to see how you like that business."

He agreed to do it, but was too restless to fall in with his uncle's next suggestion about sitting through some vaudeville, as music halls were apparently known over here. Instead he walked back to the hotel and walked up to the top floor. Here he looked down on the Fifth Avenue Promenade, but didn't find that sight soothing, either. He descended to the room that he had insisted on taking rather than to lodge with his uncle and aunt. To his own surprise, almost as soon as his head hit the pillow he fell asleep. At least there was some advantage to being unhappy on land as opposed to being at peace on the ocean.

He was startled by the offices of the New York *Ledger* as soon as he walked in. Women worked here, most of them in white blouses and dark skirts. Behind barred windows, several were taking personal advertisements, rephrasing them in brief and understandable English. Another young woman walked with him through a long line of desks at which others operated clattering typewriters. It all seemed like a prim Englishman's idea of a respectable Oriental harem.

The sight of three men in a room off to a side was more than enough to capture his attention. Two were standing. The third, badly dressed, sat on a padded, pointed-arch side chair.

"I know you promised the bluecoats not to talk about what you saw," said one of the men on his feet, reaching for an oversized pad and pencil, "but you need money or you wouldn't be here, so you can make a drawing of what you claim you saw."

"I don't draw good," said the ill-dressed man.

"An artist on our staff will do the donkey work after you get finished," the third man snapped.

Torin wished he could have stayed to hear more. Certainly a life as a newspaper staff member would be of continual interest, with its need to be perpetually alert and with no idea of what sort of work the next day might bring. It was delightful to have made such a discovery so soon after the beginning of his journey.

The girl who had been guiding him suddenly turned to her right. After passing a telephone closet, she opened a black-painted door and stepped to one side almost like a well-trained butler.

"Please make yourself comfortable, sir. Mr. Castle will be joining you shortly."

He had never been in a room like it. One wall was covered by a map of New York City. The desk, of mahogany and satinwood, was ornamented by black and white tambour doors over a network of pigeonholes. The window was three-quarters closed, making for a room that was stuffy in the best tradition.

Uncle Ferdy was cordial when he walked in, shaking hands cheerily and offering a cigar. He waved both hands around the room as if offering it to the younger man.

"And there is the *Ledger*'s domain," he said, pointing to the map on which small circles pinpointed the location of some news kiosks. "At the moment, the advertising staff is embarking on a new program to advertise the features of our paper in the pages of rival publications."

"That is distinctively forward-looking," Torin murmured pacifically.

"And we are trying to persuade the publishers to utilize the new Griggs process of photochromolithography, also, which will enhance the look of our paper if we can get his agreement to proceed. It isn't easy."

Torin winced at the notion of having to cajole some cabal of businessmen to act according to their own best interests.

"If you truly wish to learn about the distribution and sales of newspapers, I can teach you enough so that can gain employment anywhere at home, I can assure you. The problem you have brought me, Torin, will be solved."

"No, I—frankly, I would like to be in a different corner of this arena, so to speak."

Uncle Ferdy quirked his magnificent brows.

"What I would like is to be with the reporting staff of a newspaper."

"You want to be—what?" Uncle Ferdy resembled his nephew's idea of a settler in the plains whose head had just made contact with a tomahawk.

Torin repeated the salient part of what he had previously said.

"Your mother would never forgive me if I permitted that to happen," Uncle Ferdy murmured and his face whitened at the prospect of his sister's wrath. "You don't want to be a reporter, to spend your time working to produce something that only exists to provide a wrapping for the next day's fish or meat or garbage. Who would take seriously the words that appear in a vehicle that wraps a smelt?"

"You seem to have suddenly changed your point of view about this publication," Torin pointed out.

He would have added "uncle," but it seemed tacitly understood that no family title would be used between them on these premises.

"The production and sale of merchandise are serious matters, and the man who knows what is needed in order to sell one type of article can sell other types in case of need."

"I have no wish to sell the work of other people, just as I don't want to build monuments or take back ruins from Ancient Greece to Piccadilly Square. Indeed a long list could be put together of occupations of which I want no part. There is one career, however, which I think I would like to have."

"It's a terrible mistake," Uncle Ferdy persisted.

"I am sorry to be a disappointment to you."

"All that you could accomplish is to give your entire vocational life to aiding an enterprise that no one has any zeal to improve on that level. There is no vaulting ambition on anyone's part to improve the quality of the reporting."

Torin shrugged.

"Besides, everything has to be done at a certain time and in a certain way. You come in at a certain time, Torin, you do your set work, and you are subject to the decisions of others. All the decisions might be wrong or activated by envy and malice."

Torin's eyes narrowed. "But I wouldn't be entirely under someone's thumb."

"You certainly can be and would be," Uncle Ferdy went on, seeing that his nephew was disturbed at that last condition. "Sometimes you work hard at a news account and an editor doesn't allot it anything like the space you are sure it deserves. Sometimes you work hard and the work doesn't appear at all— and entirely because of the whims and caprices of one man."

Torin muttered, "You are telling me that even newspaper work offers no freedom to do the best possible job!"

"If you doubt me, you can prove it by talking to a few of our experienced reporters."

"I'd like to do that."

He joined his uncle at a vaudeville performance that night in Palmo's Opera House downtown. The players were none of them as skillful as the likes of Albert Chevalier, the Cockney Laureate, for example. The quips were no different from others he had heard at home in music halls such as the Alhambra. He was actually revolted by the performance of a muscular little woman with the unnerving capacity to keep a dozen sets of false teeth in midair at the same time.

"You're in a bad mood," Uncle Ferdy said once more. He had

made that same point over supper in what was called an oyster house. "You will surely find some outlet for your energies."

Torin had ended the daylight hours in a state of despondency he had hoped he would never again experience.

He had previously spoken to reporters on the *Ledger*, all of whom had confirmed his uncle's darkest forebodings. He had seen others quarreling with their editors about space for various news accounts. He had seen printers chip out words or sentences or entire paragraphs so that a particular account would take up only the space it had been previously offered. Worst of all, to his mind, he had heard his uncle laying down the law to one of the editors about a news account that might be wounding to the family of one of the *Ledger*'s advertising patrons.

"I think I can suggest something that will be good for you," Uncle Ferdy said cheerfully after another look at his nephew's long face. They were leaving the plush lobby of the vaudeville theatre. "Come along."

He led the way downtown to a street with a name Torin didn't catch. There was a restaurant, judging by the sign in front, into which Torin was directed. Only when they got inside did he remember that the two of them had already taken supper. Before he could say so it dawned on him that the place wasn't like any restaurant he had ever visited.

No food was on the few tables, but drinks were in plain sight. These were being served by painted young waitresses in shoddy finery and with mechanical smiles, their heads tilted coquettishly, postures winningly erect, voices pitched low. Ferdy asked for two beers and passed across four coins when these were brought to the table he had taken for himself and Torin.

"My nephew just arrived in New York City and hasn't seen too many different places," Uncle Ferdy said, with a wink at the girl. "I thought he might like to—um, see how an enterprise like this is run."

Torin was unpleasantly startled that his uncle would consider him to have the makings of a tavern keeper.

"It can sure be arranged," the girl said with a wider smile. "You're old enough, and you'll enjoy it."

"I beg your pardon," Torin said to the girl. "I thank you for the offer to guide me on an inspection of these premises—"

He didn't notice the girl's eyebrows soar almost to her hairline.

"—but I think that my uncle has misunderstood my feelings about—ah—"

"Do what you want, English, but you're missing something," the girl said. She strode away, hips swinging as if she was confident that every man stared after her.

"Uncle, how can you possibly think that a member of a family in London society would ever show the slightest interest in keeping a restaurant or tavern or whatever this place happens to be?"

"Your mind seems to work on only one track of railroad at a time," Uncle Ferdy said. It had apparently crossed his own mind that Torin was something of a dunce.

That was when Torin's eyes widened. He realized at long last that his uncle had actually wanted to offer a different sort of relaxation than he might have anticipated.

Embarrassed at having been so slow to catch up, Torin busied himself drinking beer. He stood when he was finished and left at his uncle's side. He didn't look to right or left, though, and he was silent.

Because he found himself in a continually grim mood, he decided to return home rather than tour the former Colonies. Two weeks remained until a ship reservation in the first class could be secured. He kept counting the hours until he'd be back to familiar ground.

It would have been unsettling to spend day and night in his hotel room. Not much longer than a coffin, he had decided, and about as narrow. Only by a miracle had a bed been packed against the far wall by an opened closet and a table with chair set down inches from the door. There was certainly no room for pacing. He hadn't retained any interest in the view of the Fifth Avenue Promenade from the top floor. People, carriages, and some automobiles in motion weren't nearly as restful as the view of mid-ocean from the deck of a ship.

His uncle and aunt made a point of taking him to places where he might feel at ease. He won a bet at nine-to-five odds on Scottish Chieftain for the Belmont Stakes, but the pleasure didn't last long. It was impossible to stop telling himself that he was every bit as clever as Cressida at picking out horses to win at different race meetings. Cressy was supporting the family, however, while he remained nothing more than a deadweight upon the others' finances.

And he was likely to remain a deadweight.

He found himself almost entirely confused by the sight of a baseball game several days later. His aunt had expected it to conform with cricket, but Torin was unnerved by everything from the layout of the field to the continual running. Naturally he told his aunt afterward with as much sincerity as he could muster that he had found the spectacle enthralling.

He did happen to be amused by the American insult "blatherskite," which he heard several times. It had a pleasing sound, although he couldn't imagine the likes of Benjamin Disraeli having ever used that word in the course of a debate with William Gladstone.

Of course his uncle saw to it that he was introduced to some men of business, but no help was ever offered after a brief talk about his family's finances. Nor was he particularly interested in what any of those men might have offered. He found, though, that it would take almost no money to begin as a salesman in the stock market. Selling shares to people who could lose considerable money following whatever advice he was ordered to give was only a step short of dishonesty. He was startled by that notion, never having thought of himself as brimming with rectitude.

His aunt took him shopping on the day before his departure. At the Alexander T. Stewart Department Store somewhere on Broadway, he accepted guidance in the choices of silks and shawls for Mama and Cressy. Aunt Martha felt that if the ladies didn't happen to be pleased by the accessories, they would relish the dark blue container with the printed New York City origination. Torin kept from saying that he ought therefore to bring back a number of empty containers and nothing else.

Outside the store he suddenly halted and inclined his head in respectful greetings.

Past a line of carriage horses wilting in the early summer sun of Broadway from the direction of Chambers Street, Annie Carr and her mother were strolling.

"I hope you are enjoying our city," the older woman said to

him after introductions had been performed. "Annie and I have just been sampling the delights of the nearest ice cream saloon, on Broadway and Franklin Street."

There was some more small talk and then the matrons fell back, leaving him to walk with Annie Carr.

"I hope you have become fond of our city," Miss Carr said, eyes downcast modestly. She might have been measuring her Italian lace-trimmed organdie and the high-buttoned boots as well.

"It is delightful," he said with automatic affability. "I can only regret that my visit will be over so soon. I return to London tomorrow."

"I would have expected that one of our girls would snap you up."

"I am hardly to be snapped up like some kind of food for those horses."

Miss Carr blushed, which brought out several spots on her forehead. "I mean, of course, that a British gentleman would be admired by all the ladies."

"The admiration couldn't deepen, Miss Carr. Of that much I can assure you."

"Is it rude to ask you why not?"

"No woman would want anything to do with me once she had got to know more about me."

"That isn't what I'd consider an all-out answer."

"What I don't have, Miss Carr, is money. I am unable to earn the off—ah, an income, in doing work that would satisfy me. As a result, I am the poorest (in two senses) of marriage prospects."

"Oh, I don't agree with that in the least. If a man has a good heart, it makes up for a lot that he might not like about—well, things."

"Do you think that a man worthy of the name would let a woman pay his chits?"

"That's a honest question and I think I can give a honest answer, Mr. Fleet. I don't think it makes the least nevermind who pays the bills—that's what we say in America—if two people love each other."

"Love alone does not confer upon a man the capacity to pay debts by doing work that is hard but worthwhile and congenial.

The girl's parents would be paying, as my own can only with difficulty help keep the family's heads above water."

"I still say that it don't make the difference if two people are married and they love each other."

That was impossible for him to believe. Love must be a cause of comfort and pleasure and happiness, but it couldn't change anyone's basic attitudes or the conditions that one encountered.

Would Miss Carr, talking so carefully about the grand passion, be changed by it? Was she likely to become as graceful as a swan? Would a married Annie Carr become as attractive as the luminous Miss Ellen Terry on a London stage?

Closer to home, what of his sister? Would a married Cressida undergo a change of appearance? Would she even dress more suitably, as called for at various social functions? Would she become less direct in dealing with a man if she was married to him? Would she lose her capacity to judge the winning ways of horses?

Not 'alf, she wouldn't.

Did the actual existence of love in a person's life go so far as to change that person? Was Mama a besotted female who thought of nothing else but the art of pleasing the man who had married her and fathered her children? Had she been in so continual a swoon as to forget that intense practicality that was so large a part of her nature? Certainly not.

Nor was there an alchemical transmutation in a married man who certainly loved his wife. Had love given Papa a sounder judgment in matters of business? Had it turned him into a stern patriarch who made unbreakable rules for wife and children to follow at pain of incurring his wrath?

Less than 'alf, this time.

He was realizing that love could endure with marriage but it would cause no alteration of personality or change in the surrounding world. Certainly not for him. It was a point that he had never considered till now. This discussion with Annie Carr had formed his opinion once and for all time.

And as a result, he supposed, he ought to have been grateful.

CHAPTER EIGHT

A blue-painted brougham-and-pair drew up before the gate of the most brightly lit home in all of Grosvenor Square. From this carriage, a splendidly dressed woman emerged with the help of the coachman. She was shortly joined by a gentleman whose clothes were the masculine equivalent of hers. Both proceeded through the opening gate and under an arch of evergreens mingled with hedge roses, stichwort, blue speedwell, and convolvulus in artful patterns. In good time the male and female reached the home of Sir Frederick and Lady Dorothy Waghorn.

They were to be the first of many. Carriages small and oversized, painted pitch-black or bright, made the same trip. Gentlemen and ladies exited with accustomed grace and proceeded past the gateway only to vanish from sight inside the huge house. Coachmen took each carriage to that limbo where it would wait until an order was conveyed for its presence in front of the house yet again.

Some of the adventurous younger guests appeared in the new horseless electric carriages. The men, having dispensed with coachmen, wore thick glasses and dust catchers instead of expensive livery. After returning from the familiar limbo, where the vehicles in motion frightened horses by the score, they walked back to the attractive young women waiting for them. Each couple proceeded through the gate.

It deserves to be noted that the guests had not begun arriving until close to eleven o'clock on this June night. Nearly all had attended other functions beforehand. Some had arrived from balls being given by relatives or business friends of the gentlemen. Others came from supper parties and would give a miss to the late supper that was sure to be offered at the Waghorns. A few rare souls had attended Covent Garden for a performance of the opera. In arriving so late they were paying a delicate compliment to Sir Frederick and Lady Dorothy, making it clear that they had saved the best for last.

For this unanimity, as will be seen, there was a splendid reason.

Cressida's search for Jeremy Dunster was under way from the moment she arrived at the ball with her family. While leaving her wrap in the cloakroom at the foot of the stairs she was glancing around keenly. The practice continued as her name was being mispronounced by a footman at the bottom of the stairs, by another at the first landing, and finally by the butler. She could think of no one but the peer, no one but Dunster.

Absently she spoke to the Waghorn ladies on the receiving line. Letitia seemed partly recovered, at least, from yesterday's illness. She was dressed in a warm-looking cardinal gown with full sleeves to protect her arms as well. Sensibly, too, she refrained from kissing Cressida.

Lady Dorothy noticed this guest's absentmindedness and smiled wryly. "Proceed, my dear," she said, "at your own risk."

Cressida noted quickly that Papa and Mama and Torin, who had been received before her, were busily renewing friendships among Sociables and almost certainly probing for information about the condition of the racehorses, which so many of them owned.

Deep in conversation with a male whom she had seen in the past but didn't know, stood Jeremy Dunster.

Her heart skipped a beat as she noted those unmistakable strong features roughened by the outdoors. He was listening idly to the other, but didn't look sideways to see if anyone more interesting might be near. Like Cressida herself, his lordship did nothing by halves.

She was hardly surprised that his dark formal clothes had been cut perfectly. For one of the few times in life she wondered whether one of her own outfits, in this case the pale yellow, showed her off to best possible effect.

It wasn't enough of a worry to keep her from carrying out the plan on which she had decided in the family carriage. If he didn't see her first, she would make a point of walking in front of him.

She would glance significantly in such a way as to meet his superb light gray eyes with their irises that were almost similarly colored.

She couldn't possibly know in advance what would happen between them after she was recognized. The forthcoming developments might start a great adventure.

The northeast end of the ballroom, where Dunster was to be found, seemed almost as far off as Land's End from John O'Groats. The number of guests between her and the goal were enough to make the walk of greater duration. By moving quickly and casting her eyes down toward her shiny pointy-tipped white shoes, she made more progress than might have been the case otherwise. Every so often it was necessary to speak with an acquaintance, but she said no more than half a dozen well-chosen words, then smiled and walked off without apologies.

She was soon close enough to hear the man in conversation with Dunster clear his throat and say in a high voice, "That fellow, Gilbert, with his Bab Ballads, he could've reformed the country through laughter had he taken that idea into his head. As it is, Jemmy, I feel that more time is needed."

Jeremy Dunster had turned away from her direction, certainly by accident as he hadn't been looking at anyone other than his companion. It would be necessary to walk yet another dozen steps, then turn to her left.

She had taken eight of those steps and was no more than thirty paces from the goal when a familiar voice could be heard.

"There are no dance partners written down on your card, Cress."

Cressida had disdained making several entries on her dance card to show that she would be busy for a certain part of the evening, whether or not that was true.

"I didn't want to take time for such nonsense, Amaryllis," she said truthfully to her friend.

Amaryllis Wyse had planted herself before Cressida. Walking off immediately would have been an act of unspeakable rudeness.

"You look lovely," Cressida said feelingly.

Amaryllis was wearing turquoise with a rich and deftly set-in trimming of embroidered lace and pearls. A design of 'mum petals had been brocaded perfectly just above the midriff.

"And your hair is done exquisitely."

This, like Cressida's own, was parted in the middle. Amaryllis's dark crown was pulled back in large waves to a high coil, however, and ornamented as well by a triple twist of pearls.

In return, and perhaps not as sincerely, Amaryllis made several complimentary remarks about the pale yellow.

Amenities had been followed by now, so it was apparently possible for Cressida to proceed amiably toward her goal.

Amaryllis drew out a hand, keeping her in place. "There are two wealthy Scottish peers in the room, but one is older than Keir Hardie and the other is already married. He, however, and despite the presence of his wife, appears to be shopping for what he would roguishly call a *petite amie.*"

Amaryllis in a gossiping mood was a source of pleasure and amusement. The rule wasn't invariable, however. Cressida did not feel in the mood to hear high points from the dossiers of various ornaments of the Empire, no matter how wealthy.

"If I wanted to torture either of those gentlemen, your information would be of value."

"I thought you'd be interested to know for a fact that I have been here long enough to perform several reconnaissances of the terrain."

"No doubt you have, Amaryllis. Now if you will permit me to do so on my own . . ."

"I can save you some time, Cress. Among the others present is Sir Kelly O'Fearguise. He is only a bart., and an Irish bart. at that. But I must add that he has nearly enough of the necessary to make him a suitable partner for an expedition to the altar at St. Peter's in Eaton Square."

"I expect that someone will surely introduce me to him before the evening is over."

"If the Irish origin is a difficulty for you, too, Cress . . ."

"It wouldn't be."

". . . then I can tell you that tonight's attendees include several unmarried men of impeccable British lineage. There is an O.B.E., a K.C.M.Q., an M.R.C.P., and an M.F.H. All of them are possible, although none is perfectly suitable."

"In that case, we might put them all together into some sort of alphabet soup."

Amaryllis, although not lacking in humor, didn't usually understand the light sallies of others. This time she blinked and nodded to cover her confusion.

"Now that I am sufficiently encouraged to hear of your researches," Cressida smiled, "excuse me while I proceed to act upon them."

Amaryllis, having looked to one side in her recent puzzlement, stiffened as she turned back. "For your own good, Cress, you must not have any congress with Jemmy Dunster."

" 'For my own good'?"

"I have no wish to see a loyal friend limping through the balance of her life in need of money to entertain members of the Diplomatic over a weekend or to give a ball. Within a few years, you and your future husband would be taken on excursions to Epping Forest by the Salvation Army in their efforts to alleviate the lot of the poor."

"Even if I married Lord Dunster, and there isn't any sign of such a possibility at the moment . . ."

"You are setting your chapeau for Jemmy Dunster, I can tell that much. Furthermore, I recall our discussion about him in this same house not forty-eight hours ago. I explained that his income was only just adequate (Didn't I say that?), and if he had a bad year of racing, you would surely find yourself sleeping on the same pallet with one of his horses. (At least I said something like *that*, I'm sure.)"

"*I* was going to say that even if I did choose to marry him, our situation would not be what you describe."

"Cress, I don't want to see you taking the risk of future difficulties of that sort."

Cressida wouldn't have put it past this friend to come between herself and Dunster, to interrupt any discussion, intrude on any courtship ritual. If a marriage ceremony were to take place and the minister asked whether anyone knew why these two hearts should not be united, it was Amaryllis Wyse who might very well offer an objection. In this matter, Amaryllis could be counted on to take the line of least assistance.

Cressida preferred to resolve the difference immediately, but it was likely to take more time than she could spare. This was another of those situations in which a person had to be discreet, be roundabout, even pretend to give in.

She turned away and walked pointedly in the opposite direction. She had decided upon a different destination to reach urgently before she did anything else.

Torin was standing with two dull-faced men, one of them telling what was probably a dull story. Torin didn't look as if he minded.

That was a clear-cut example of his sweetness of character, which made others smile contentedly in his presence. Small wonder that as a child he had never hesitated to give his young sister his dissected pictures, drum and alphabet blocks, wooden animals, even his hobby horse. Charmer as he had always been, he had become more so since his return from Yankeeland less than a year ago.

He apologized to the dull-faced speaker with a smile and a rueful shrug shortly after being gestured to one side by his sister.

"Torin, since I've grown up I have rarely asked for a great favor, but I am asking now. You must, you absolutely must, do this for me."

And in the fewest possible words she told him exactly what she wanted.

CHAPTER NINE

Only a few minutes were required before Cressida was able to look across the room and see that Amaryllis was in a conversation that she found absorbing. Miss Wyse must have checked her usual first impulse to leave the presence of any young male who wasn't endowed with a more-than-ample supply of money.

Torin, however, would have been charming and straightforward from the beginning. Whatever the subject, he would speak with his usual sincerity.

It wasn't at all unsettling that as soon as the musicians struck up a waltz, Amaryllis joined Torin on the dance floor.

Cressida delayed no longer.

"I know that we have met," said Lord Jeremy Dunster in that thrillingly deep voice she remembered so well. "Perhaps you recall me."

At long, long last he was facing her. His eyes had been ensnared, and he had strode away from his male companion. He stood with his usual superb posture, jacket and vest buttoned formally, and showing no effect of the June night heat.

"We met in Cheshire," she said, cheeks flaming at the recollection of the kiss that he had briefly bestowed on her with such unexpectedness. "You were racing Lover's Knot that day."

"Which won."

True enough, but she didn't like being reminded.

"No one can always predict which horse will emerge triumphant, as you must be aware. In the case of Lover's Knot, I was mistaken."

"A certain amount of work is needed to make deductions from a horse's condition," he observed reasonably. Then he added, "It is inadvisable to be convinced that a horse will win—or lose—because of the name that has been given to it."

"I did no such thing, as you may recollect."

"You offered reasons that may have been influenced by the animal's color, for all I know."

Cressida flushed to the roots of her blond hair, as if there was so much as a syllable of truth in what he was saying about her.

"You do understand that I am not imputing blame to you or condemning you. But it is difficult to imagine that a young woman like yourself, a woman of family wealth and (I believe) some position among the Sociables of London, would choose to do anything else."

"In-deed!"

She had spoken during a pause in the music, and her voice carried. The player with the bass viol looked as if his eyes would pop out with shock. One violinist's jaw dropped almost to his collar. The harpist was surprised enough to let go of his instrument. The trumpeter, preparing to unleash what he must have fondly imagined were musical notes, resembled a lion who sees its prey in sight but is unable to effect a capture.

"It is not my scorn that you arouse, but my pity," his lordship said, offering the last consolation that Cressida could have wanted. "To think of someone who attends race meetings but understands nothing about those glorious animals, their intelligence, their love of victory."

"I do understand," Cressida responded through teeth clenched by fury. It seemed incredible that her unfortunate evaluation of one animal remained vivid, but the warmth of their previous talk and even the quick but memorable kiss appeared to have been forgotten by him. As far as the first point was concerned, it was impossible to tell him that her capacity to choose winning horses in advance of a race was all that had kept her family from the clutches of the poorhouse.

She spoke sternly before he could launch himself into further discourse. "I did not seek you out for a lecture about the character of horses. Another man would have been aware of that on the instant."

"Of course you are quite right, Miss—Miss Cressida Fleet. Jemmy Dunster has been exposed as a boor and a man whose vocation has come perilously close to an obsession. Will you show pity by permitting me to inflict myself upon you on the dance floor?"

So there was some humor in him. Perhaps a further interest, entirely aside from his handsomeness, could be justified.

"Thank you, Lord Dunster. It may be assumed that my Mama will approve of this gallant endeavor."

Mama would certainly have given her consent to one dance with a peer. Dunster didn't look at all like the stable lad for whom he had apparently been taken back at Cheshire. Clothes and surroundings made the ultimate difference in judging another, a point that she was not the first to discern.

Cressida rested an arm on his, happily aware of firmness and strength. She could probably have been raised from the floor by that arm alone. The notion brought a fierce blush to her cheeks.

A dance between them was not to take place. At least not immediately.

The double doors had swung wide for the first time. All eyes turned as a dozen arrivals trooped into the room by two's. Judging from the astonishment displayed by the hostess and her daughter, the presence of these guests had been totally unexpected.

One of the first pairs to enter was none other than the portly and bearded Albert Edward, Prince of Wales. Among his titles were those of Duke of Saxe Coburg and Gotha, Duke of Cornwall and Rothesay, Earl of Chester and Carrick and Dublin, Baron of Renfrew and Lord of the Isles, Great Steward of Scotland, Knight of the Elephant of Denmark, Knight of the Golden Fleece, Knight of the White Elephant of Siam, and Bailli Grand Cross of the order of St. John of Jerusalem.

Most of his other titles applied only to the British establishment. He was an army field marshal, as well as colonel-in-chief of the three regiments of household cavalry; Colonel of the Tenth Hussars; Captain-General and Colonel of the Honorable Artillery Company; military aide-de-camp to the Queen; Captain in the Royal Naval Reserve; Honorary Colonel of the Oxford and Cambridge and Middlesex Civil Service Corps of rifle volunteers; Colonel of the Royal Aberdeenshire Highlanders; Colonel of the Sutherland Highland Rifle Volunteers; and Colonel of the Blucher Hussars.

His remaining titles did not involve the military. He was Elder Brother of Trinity House; Grand Master of the United Grand Lodge of Freemasons of England; Barrister-at-law and bencher of the Middle Temple; and President of the Society of Arms. Oxford had honored him with a D.C.L., and Cambridge and Trinity College in Dublin had each honored him with an LL.D.

He was, of course, first in line to succeed his mother to the throne of England.

Another title was not official. His persistent successes with women other than the Princess had resulted in the sardonic sobriquet of Edward the Caresser. While the other titles had been grafted on him, the latter recognition had been well and truly earned.

At his side, looking lovely in black that almost fit like a robe of ermine, was his princess. Every female witness, having favorably judged the Princess's gown and coif, asked herself whether after all these years the Princess still looked more Danish than British. No collective answer was offered.

The Prince smiled as the Waghorn females curtseyed in unison. "I decided," he said in a surprisingly clear voice, "to inflict myself upon you very briefly."

"Your Royal Highness, we are honored that you have chosen to pay this visit."

His Royal Highness nodded. Everyone knew that he had impulsively made other such appearances, more often when unaccompanied by his princess. Perhaps he conceived himself sometimes as British exemplar of the tradition of the Caliph of Bagdad.

"I am here to acknowledge your kindness in giving this ball to benefit the Association for Aid to the Improvident Ill."

The Waghorn ladies curtseyed yet again. This time Miss Letitia's face turned a muddy gray because of her recent illness.

The music resumed after a signal from Lady Waghorn. The Prince and Princess had taken to the dance floor by themselves.

At the conclusion of the waltz, Princess Alexandra dispatched one of her ladies in waiting to request a dance from the husband of her hostess. Sir Frederick Waghorn agreed delightedly. When that polka was done, the Princess ordered another of her ladies to request a dance from a peer with whom she was acquainted. Both men were shortly joining the royalty on the floor with other partners.

The Prince, for his part, danced with Lady Waghorn and then with Letitia, keeping a distance with the daughter because she clearly showed traces of an indisposition. His duty done, the Prince was free to send an equerry to any young woman whose appearance pleased him.

Cressida and Dunster, like the other witnesses, had been respectfully silent for the first few minutes after the royal arrival. As soon as Albert Edward and his Alexandra took to the dance floor, however, an onslaught of music made it possible to whisper without moving the head.

"I will have five horses at Kent over the weekend," Dunster said after a moment in a whisper that was fully as stirring to the senses as his normal speech. His mind had returned to a consid-

eration of the joys of racing, as no other subject presented itself
to form an outlet for his energies.

"I have seen the lists," Cressida informed him.

"Three victories will be mine, and I can tell you which horses to
wager on."

"Thank you so much."

"You sound dubious about my judgment of the animals."

"It would surprise me to see three victories from those
horses."

A new voice intruded calmly.

"Pardon me."

The well-dressed stranger's face was filled out by the afteref-
fects of too much food. A great quantity of drink allied to sleep-
less nights had helped form a network of red lines across the
whites of his eyes. This man's life had been given over to dissipa-
tion of various sorts.

"Pardon me, miss," he said, clearing smoke out of his lungs as
best he could. "His Royal Highness requests the pleasure of the
next dance with you."

Until that moment, Cressida had been the happiest girl in the
ballroom. She had finally dragooned Jemmy Dunster after a great
expenditure of time, and after hurdling several difficult barriers.
Not only did they share an interest in horses, but an admiration
for each other. Should they be unable to join on the dance floor
until the royals had left, they would be deep in conversation at
each other's side. Perhaps they would be touching.

But now, someone wanted to tear her away from his side,
almost surgically. Even though it was the Prince of Wales himself
who virtually commanded that she dance with him, the straightforward Cressida was angered by the intrusion. An impartial
observer might have felt that she was outraged.

She gave her answer calmly, however. "Please inform His
Royal Highness that I would be honored to dance with him—"

"Kindly follow me."

"—at some later occasion."

The stranger's brows soared almost to his hairline. "You are
refusing to dance with His Royal Highness?"

She wanted to say that under no circumstances could she take
pleasure in the opportunity to dance with a gross older man

whose sins were revolting to contemplate. Tact, although it didn't come easily to her, was far more advisable.

"No, I am gratefully accepting His Royal Highness's invitation with, however, a condition."

"I beg your pardon for the intrusion in His Highness's name," said the stranger, choking only slightly. "I shall inform him immediately of your decision."

She was aware of murmurs behind her. Words of delighted horror must have been forming on the lips of various ladies and being transmitted from one to another in recounting the incident. There had probably been no greater reversal of expectations since the summer of '86. The occasion had been far from social, Mr. Gladstone having come to Blenheim Palace to tender his resignation as Prime Minister. In doing so, his feet had encountered a carpet and he very nearly tripped. It had been widely whispered afterward that Queen Victoria was amused.

Cressida did not look around until she heard a woman call out and the thud that followed. The difficulty had been caused by Mrs. Anna Marshwood, whose nouveau riche husband had sought a mention on the honors list for these twenty years. Hearing about a young woman who spurned the company of the Prince of Wales had caused that good lady to swoon where she stood.

CHAPTER TEN

The Fleet family ought to have been contented, by and large, on the carriage ride back home to Albemarle Street from the charity ball. Mrs. Fleet had been told in confidence that the famous horse Rondelay had performed badly at a trial run. Mr. Fleet knew for a fact that Tiddler was not going to run at Newmarket in October.

Both items would be of help in forecasting the winners of important set-to's on the turf.

As for Torin, he had been offered no information but seemed happily dazed, smiling at nothing apparent and closing his eyes as if to imagine some sight that couldn't be visualized by other mortals.

Cressida, too, had cause for happiness. True, she had been rushed off home only a few minutes after the difficulty caused by Wales. Before that, however, she felt certain that a silent understanding had been reached with Dunster. There was feeling between the two of them and it could increase in intensity.

The Fleets, however, collectively and individually, were far from contented.

Torin and Cressida were unsettled because of the heated discussion between Cressida and her mother. Mr. Fleet was disturbed primarily by the volume of sound that was being generated.

"You shall not attend another function without my keeping a sharp eye on you at all times," Mama said, having made that practical decision after only a few minutes of recrimination.

"Nothing that I did was wrong," Cressida pointed out, for perhaps the ninth time. "Nothing immoral."

"One doesn't refuse a dance with the Prince of Wales," said Mama inflexibly. "Not unless one wishes to be a source of laughter or condemnation or both."

The argument went on with each of the participants making the same points over and over. No longer an argument, let alone a discussion, the talk became a verbal equal of one of those thaumatrope discs from Cressida's childhood. The disc would be spun and the same riddle was posed every time.

Mr. Fleet didn't talk about the matter until after the family had left their carriage and gone listlessly into their respective rooms in Albemarle Street. He joined his wife in the back drawing room not long afterward. Taking the Tavistock easy chair and putting both feet up on the settee, he lighted a favorite pipe with one of his phosphorus matches and spoke of the matter on both their minds.

"You know, it may be just as well that Cressy didn't have a dance with Wales—ah, shocking though it seems, of course."

From her facing position on the Mogadore chair, Mrs. Fleet asked icily, "And why is it just as well?"

"You know what sort of a reputation Wales has with the ladies, the young girls. It is hard to be sure that a cloistered female confronted with so famous a man might not have been overwhelmed and done something unwise at a later time."

"For appearance's sake, she could have acted in a way that is socially desirable and then forgotten this entire matter of dancing with Wales or anyone else if she didn't want to."

"Perhaps she had a reason for not dancing with Wales."

"A reason?" Mrs. Fleet was outraged. "A reason to go against all common sense, to bring all eyes to her in a critical way? A reason?"

"At no time did you ask her such a question."

"I have far better things to do with my time," she said icily.

Her husband felt as if he had broken at least two of the commandments at the same time. He absorbed himself in experiencing the aroma of pipe smoke while he inspected the contents of the *Financial Day*. What fortunes could his own father have wrested by acting on some of the information contained on the printed sheets?

Gladys Fleet hadn't been inattentive to the reasonable objection that her husband had raised. She felt that it contained another conversational weapon to turn upon the benighted Cressy.

"And might I ask *why* you chose to ignore the offer from Wales?" she asked over the veal croquettes at the following night's supper table. She spoke quietly so that Mrs. Durbin, the housekeeper, on the other side of the opened door, wouldn't hear.

Cressida maneuvered the parsley, which obscured a section of the meat, and said, "I was speaking to another."

"And why, if I might ask, was he of more importance to you than making a fool of yourself?"

"I was speaking to Lord Jeremy Dunster, who trains his own horses before racing them."

Mr. Fleet, alerted, put in, "Yes, he had Lover's Knot at Cheshire, if I'm not mistaken."

Cressida had been preoccupied with her recollections of the brief but thrilling moments close to his lordship. Now she realized that the freshly burgeoning argument might be nipped in the bud.

"Lord Dunster was about to tell me which of his horses would be going into their next races in first-rate condition."

Mama immediately created a distraction, raising her voice toward the opened door. "Mrs. Durbin, will you please take this animal out of here?"

She was referring to the russet bulldog, which had ventured amiably into the dining room, a foray that no family members generally minded. This was a friendly beast named Clinical after a horse that Cressida had picked at Goodwood, and which had won handily. As a result, the family had earned considerable pounds and shillings and pence.

Mama waited until the dog had been dispatched and Mrs. Durbin was back at her station near the opened door.

"I have to agree that a ticklish problem was posed," Mama conceded, not without reluctance. "But it is also true that you could have returned to his lordship after the dance with Wales."

"I had no way of being certain he would wait for me."

"The risk was worth taking, as Torin will agree. You are more willing to listen to your brother than to she who gave you birth, I sometimes think. Torin, please tell your sister what she should have done—Torin!"

It didn't seem as if he had heard. Torin was sitting slackly at table for once. His portion of veal croquettes was still mostly hidden by off-color parsley. His usually firm chin had been drawn back, and those bright blue eyes were clouded over.

"What is wrong with you, Torin?" Mama asked sharply, astonished at not hearing the usual immediate acknowledgment from him. "Are you ill or moonstruck?"

Cressida's attention had been wandering, but now she turned curiously. Her feelings about Jemmy Dunster made it clear that there could be only one reason for Torin's particular air of bemusement. Her brother had not wished for marriage or love until he could be in control of his own finances, but that sterling resolution had wavered. Clearly, from the sight of him, Torin was in love.

With whom?

The only possible answer occurred immediately to Cressida, but she didn't believe it.

CHAPTER ELEVEN

Amaryllis Wyse stepped out of the hansom cab into a working-class street she'd never before had any occasion to visit. If the cabbie protested in order to get more money than had been agreed on at the outset, she would pay without demur. While she was on Baker Street, she didn't want to be noticed.

Even as she took the necessary walk to her destination, Amaryllis found herself thinking admiringly about Torin Fleet. He had been quite wonderful at the Waghorns' charity ball. His recent trip to America seemed to have changed him for the better. Perhaps, unlike so many young men, he was no longer trying to impress others with proofs of his wealth and position. That would make him a decided novelty. He had only wanted to be the best of company. In that, he had achieved a brilliant success.

At the building she sought, the spry landlady pointed to the upstairs door of that tenant with whom Amaryllis was determined to consult. Gripping the wall with a cautious palm, she took the first steps.

The correct door opened to her knock.

"And here, if I mistake not, is our client now," said the hawk-nosed man who greeted her. "Miss Wyse? Please enter. This is my friend and confidant, the doctor. You may speak freely before him."

She had entered a room like no other in her experience. A strong odor of tobacco was everywhere. Glass vials dangled from a fixture above a scarred table. One of the walls appeared to have been defaced by a pattern of bullets. If Amaryllis hadn't already been so upset, she would have shuddered without restraint.

As she removed her cape and smoothed down the black satin dress, the hawk-nosed man looked intently at her. Before she could feel even more unsettled, his next remark came. It was totally disarming.

"I see that you have fallen upon hard times."

"What makes you think that?"

"Elementary, Miss Wyse. Although your dress speaks of comfortable circumstances, the blacking on your kid boots is Scientific Shine, which is used by those in want of money."

He couldn't have known that Amaryllis had instructed her maid to use no other product on those kid boots. Scientific Shine was most effective in bringing out a high sheen. In these circumstances, it would be best to humor him.

"You are most extraordinary, sir, to know that much about me."

"I am currently preparing a monograph that will instruct investigators what may be learned from various grades of shoe blacking." Another keen look. "I observe, too, that you are in the throes of a romance. One of your gloves was put on inside out and you have not yet removed either of them."

"Indeed—I, yes, that may be so." Was it Amaryllis Wyse speaking like a schoolgirl in *The Mikado?* "That fact may be said, sir, to have brought me here."

The gentleman who had been introduced as the doctor looked admiringly at his companion.

"Two hits!" he exclaimed. "Two palpable hits!"

"Contain yourself, my dear fellow! Now, Miss Wyse, kindly tell us your problem. Speak frankly and omit no detail however slight."

"I am here because of—well, Cress is a great friend as well as the sister of the young man—well, a certain young man. I have been worried about Cress and had decided to consult someone who might help. Last night's happenings made the matter far more urgent, I can assure you."

"But what, pray, is the exact difficulty?"

"Cress—Cressida, my friend—is obsessed with wagering upon horse racing. The compulsion causes her to act against her own best interests. You will more fully appreciate the dilemma when I tell you that last night she preferred to speak with a horse owner rather than to dance with the Prince of Wales."

"And what do you want me to do?"

"See to it that she is brought back to herself, that she does not attempt to marry a horse owner whose ability to support her must be imperiled if a season passes during which a large number of his animals do not win in their contests. Cress would find herself virtually a pauper."

"Hmmm! Upon reflection, I do not see this as a problem that involves, say, a secret treaty."

"Pardon?"

"If such a document were to fall into the wrong hands, the peace of the very world could be imperiled," he explained.

"No, nothing like that," Amaryllis had to agree.

"Nor does the matter concern a hound stalking the moors and killing all and sundry who venture into its path."

"No hound."

"To say nothing of, as a further example, anarchists being involved. Nor is there a league of men with red hair, although I trust I am sufficiently open-minded to accept blond hair as an alternate. No such factors enter into this problem you pose."

"No such factors at all."

"If your problem contained any element that was bizarre or outré, Miss Wyse, I would leap to your assistance. However, I am a consulting detective, and the only one in London. A problem of romance, even compounded by obsession, is perforce beyond my ken."

Amaryllis felt stricken. "Is there nothing to be done?"

The doctor cleared his throat. "I never intrude upon my friend's prospective clients, but I can possibly be of assistance in this type of difficulty."

The consulting detective looked offended at first and then drew himself up. "I suggest that you and Miss Wyse discuss the situation whilst I lull my mind by emulating Pablo Sarasate."

And he drew up a violin from the mantel. He played in a manner that he must have fondly hoped was worthy of the great Spanish soloist. Amaryllis, even as she understood the sensible advice being offered, couldn't help hearing that the consulting detective played abominably.

Outside, as she called for a hansom, she glanced around. Her eye was held by the sight of three men and a heavily painted woman gathered at the southwest corner of Baker Street. They were watching a constable in shiny blue serge, with a heavy stick and a whistle on a rope around his neck. The constable was strapping an unconscious man into one of the hand ambulances that still dotted the city's middle-class and poor areas. The two wheels swayed slightly as he tested those straps securing the scrawny man's chest and midriff and thigh. A shade that was supposed to cover the unfortunate's head from the elements wobbled as the constable reached for twin handles and raised one end of the vehicle.

The nearest hansom couldn't pull up quickly enough to suit Amaryllis.

CHAPTER TWELVE

By the time he was ten years old, Kenneth Baldro had already resembled nothing so much an undertaker condoling with the relatives of the deceased. At the age of twenty, he could have passed for a physician telling some patient's closest relatives that the only remaining hope was to put one's trust in a Higher Power. There seemed no doubt that Kenneth Baldro was going to be engaged in one profession or the other.

He had decided early enough upon a career as a doctor. Dutifully he had been a good student who performed capably at school and in his practice—for a while.

He discovered that the actual work was often defaced by an unseemly air of optimism. Male patients were usually trying to put a good face on their complaints. Women whose indispositions caused them to take laudanum almost by the quart would turn away smiling when he came into view. Even children seemed not to see the dark side of the most minor irritation. One did not, after all, symbolically draw up blankets over the head of a patient who suffered from the collywobbles.

Baldro changed his work area, going into research. Surely an air of proper gloom would prevail in the laboratory where matters of life and death were everyday occurrences. Soon enough it became clear that when the chemists were not at work they were inexplicably given to playing practical jokes on one another.

He resigned in dismay, convinced that there seemed no natural outlet in which to exercise his birth-gift for conveying portentousness and gloom. It was beginning to seem as if his worst fears were coming true and he could look forward to nothing but a future filled to the brim with good cheer and hope.

Only because he continued reading medical journals (so as to learn about any forthcoming plague) did he discover that his quest could yet end in a holy grail of sorts.

A new discipline had been unleashed on the medical world by some great visionary in far-off Vienna. It was this doctor's hope to aid those who were not medically ill but suffered from brain agonies. An opportunity was offered for others, not only for practitioners in *Alt Wien*, to deal with people whose problems might happily—from the vantage of someone with his gloomy temperament—prove intractable.

Baldro had embarked upon the study of hypnosis, the detailed consideration of highly specialized papers conceived in German, and the calculating of fees. Surely a grim future beckoned, posing exactly the sort of professional situation in which he would at last feel comfortable.

"And you tell me that the young woman is a slave to wagering?"

"That is so," Amaryllis said.

She was seated comfortably in Kenneth Baldro's Harley Street chambers. This was the vicinity in which the best medical practitioners in Britain could be located. That knowledge was soothing. She had begun to relax from the moment she saw the building with its patterned brick walls and tiny turrets and pointed arches above rounded first-floor windows. Why, it was almost like a residence!

Baldro folded his hands in contemplation. The alienist was in his thirties, with dark hair, thick brows, and heavy-lidded brown eyes in a sharp face. A serious-minded man, apparently, who didn't play the violin or talk admiringly about secret treaties.

"And you tell me that she may wed a man who would do much harm to her?"

"She is enamored of a peer who is likely to suffer ill luck with the horses he owns and trains for most of his livelihood. There will be at least one difficult season for him, perhaps several in succession. Such a course of events might well cause my friend to become impoverished."

"Or to become an inmate of Colney Hatch if her nerves cannot accommodate such a change." Kenneth Baldro wondered how a case of this type would be dealt with in Vienna, the fountain of knowledge. "But why do you concern yourself so closely with the matter? I certainly understand and sympathize with the demands of friendship. Such an active interest as you show, however, seems more than is to be expected even of so good a cause."

"It could be that I may come to consider marrying into her family. The Fleets are moderately well-to-do, but if one member becomes impoverished, then it seems obvious that all the others will be affected—and their marital connections, too."

"An emergency is in the making," said the alienist, rubbing his hands to anticipate his treatment of the case. "Very well. I will see the lady."

This announcement, far from causing gratification, appeared to offer a source of difficulty. Amaryllis Wyse flinched.

"She's not here."

"I realize that. An appointment will remedy the difficulty to which you refer."

"I had hoped you might tell me what to do in order to help her."

"My dear young lady!" The alienist was properly scandalized at the notion of somebody being of assistance who was not in the position to levy a fee. "You are hardly able to implement such advice, not being an alienist yourself. This matter calls for a professional laying on of hands, so to speak."

"But I cannot tell her of it or she will be furious at my having gone behind her back. I—what is to be done?"

"Only one solution presents itself," Baldro said evenly. "I must have an interview with her during some social situation, one in which she is not aware of my profession and its application to her tragic circumstances."

"And then?"

"I will persuade her to submit herself to treatment."

"Do you think you can?"

The alienist pursed his lips in annoyance that a pronouncement of his might be questioned by someone who was not a practitioner of his vocation.

"Cress," said her friend finally, "will be at the race meeting at Foxbridge in Kent this Saturday."

"In that case, I will be in Kent, too. You, Miss Wyse, will act as my escort."

Amaryllis didn't flinch this time, nor did she find herself in any transport of happiness. She imagined Torin's face flushed with anger when he saw another man in her company. He might not immediately realize why Baldro had been brought there, and could become difficult. True, there was as yet no understanding between them, but Amaryllis felt that there was reason to hope.

Nevertheless, the wisdom of her own mama would be acceptable in this dilemma. In for a penny, as Mrs. Wyse occasionally muttered resignedly, in for a pound.

"Very well," Amaryllis consented, and wished that the weekend was over. She couldn't help suddenly asking herself if any good was likely to come out of it after all.

CHAPTER THIRTEEN

Cressida had no reason to be aware of the impending interview. She was actually smiling to herself as the family carriage passed that celebrated double line of sun-flecked linden trees leading to the Foxbridge racecourse. Such a double line had at one time proclaimed an estate owner's Whig sympathies, the tradition reaching back to the days of William the Third. Currently, it proclaimed only that the course area had originally been part of an estate whose owner had fallen upon difficult times.

She didn't regret having to leave her dust cloak behind in the carriage. Rarely had she looked more appealing. For the occasion of the meeting with Dunster, which was certain to take place, she had put on the white hopsacking with its delft-blue bias folds, and a simple straw boater deliciously tilted on her head. The man who could refrain from being attracted by the sight would have had to be far more single-minded even than Jeremy Dunster.

She told the family, "I intend to stroll about for a few minutes and listen to any talk that might be helpful."

Papa was thinking only about the family's wagers. "We have to get in our bets very soon, Cressy."

Torin looked as if his mind was elsewhere. He had ventured to speak quietly to his sister about the prodigious charms of Miss Amaryllis Wyse. Clearly he was smitten. It seemed doubtful that a wedding would result, considering that young lady's strongly held view about proceeding to the altar only at the side of a man with the wealth of Croesus.

Mama was the only family member whose plans were altered by Cressida's announced jaunt. "I will accompany you."

Having expected no less, Cressida was not averse to the plan. A meeting with Jemmy might be impressive for Mama, too. Jemmy

might habitually be a tad more absorbed than necessary in the
successes of his animals, but he was indisputably handsome. The
sight of him would be enough to melt an older woman's heart.
Mama tapped at specks of dust on her walking dress, keeping
sensibly busy while in motion. "At least you won't be able to
spend time in talk with some owner about airy nothings. That, I
strongly suspect, is what you did at the Waghorns'."

Cressida's face must have revealed too much on the night in
question as it was probably doing now. She'd never been able to
keep relevant information from Mama—or, if truth be told, from
almost anybody else.

Turning away to hide a blush, she was nearly knocked over by a
large fat man who wore one ring on his every pudgy finger. In the
baking sun, the man's oversized hat gleamed.

"I recall an older man saying to me once," Mama remarked
meditatively, "that the shabbier the gent, the more decorations
he would wear and the more he glittered."

Such wisdom might have been questioned by Amaryllis Wyse,
among others. All the same, it would be preferable if Jemmy
Dunster was not dressed to the nines.

She realized now that she had been ignoring the common
sense that told her not to expect a sight of Dunster among the
public on a day on which one or more of his horses were racing. It
had to be enough, at this moment, to distinguish red-and-white
stable colors on one of the pennants just above the highest level
of seating space. He couldn't be far off.

A gentleman stepped smilingly in front of Mama, and asked
after her and the family. About Cressida he remarked that she
looked more like her mama every day. This was apparently considered to be complimentary.

Returning his attention to Mama, he said jovially, "What a pity
that we cannot see each other more often."

"Oh, draw it mild!" Mama said, descending for once to a near-
vulgarism. "We're too old for larks now, and I suspect that you
for one always were."

The gentleman, who looked as if he had been withered by
constant fretfulness, couldn't help saying weakly, "I can recall
when you enjoyed my presence."

"Only as someone to make large eyes at," Mama responded

briskly. "At my present age, I no longer have to waste time at such foolishness."

The gentleman tried to put a good face on this short shrift. After a small smile and a muttered remark, he left hurriedly.

"One of those who would never marry, but considers that the choice was only some female's loss and not his at all," Mama snapped as she and Cressida proceeded. "Most importantly, he can offer no useful information at this time."

That was when Mama directed a more-than-usually probing look at her potentially erring daughter.

"I take it that you took this peculiar time to go for a stroll because you were in hopes of seeing or speaking with some certain male."

It was a shrewd assumption, and Cressida was not one to deny truth.

"I can hardly refuse a dance with Wales when I'm at the racing course," she pointed out. "Nor can I get into trouble with a man."

"You could make a rendezvous to get into trouble at a later date."

"I will not do anything of that sort."

Mama nodded after a moment. More than most, she knew full well that her daughter's word could be trusted.

"Then it is only fairness itself to say that your behavior is thoughtless. No one knows whether or not you wish to bet on the outcome of the first contest. As a result, we are all on the hooks."

There was more than enough justification for Mama's attitude.

"I see no predictable winner for the first race, but I do favor Quickstep in the second."

"Very well, then. Come with me to inform your papa and brother, and then the four of us will make bets."

"Please excuse me, Mama, but I wish to stand here. I promise that I will not stir except to return to you and the others."

She was facing the track, but more important to her was the structure at the far side. This was the castellated sandstone and brick clubhouse. Through the entrance, bordered by red roses, hidcote lavender, and snowline white roses as well, Jemmy Dunster would eventually emerge. She would not have let herself be moved by anything short of main force.

Hardly had Mama walked off, glancing behind only once, than Cressida heard a familiar female voice.

"Cress!"

She could hardly keep from turning. In a pigeon's-throat promenade costume and a hesitant smile across curving lips, was Amaryllis Wyse.

And at Amaryllis's side stood a stranger who was obviously her escort.

Cressida's immediate reaction was to think back to an incident that had involved her papa's guv'nor. Sir Whitman Fleet had been accepted by all as a man of his word, a man who could be fierce toward those who had made promises and not kept them. Having promised to play with her after supper at his house, he could be expected to keep his word.

Sir Whitman had got up from table in the midst of a discussion about some daub by the French painter Corot and hadn't come back after the finish of supper.

Young Cressida ventured into his study, planning to remind Sir Whitman of his promise. He was seated very heavily in the best chair. His heavy-lidded eyes, half open, looked more than usually time-weakened. There seemed more veins on the backs of his hands. His face had reddened and he breathed with enormous difficulty. The eyes closed suddenly and his body moved forward.

Most vividly of all to her recollection, Cressida had thought that he had broken his promise to play with her. Several days later, when tactfully told that Sir Whitman had gone away to join the angels in heaven she had felt certain that he'd only done it to avoid facing her after such treachery.

Although Amaryllis was closer to hand, Cressida's feelings were the same. This friend had virtually indicated much interest in a young man who seemed equally attracted. Now she turned around and came to a place where he must be among those present, but in the company of another.

There were limits to civilized behavior.

Amaryllis had transgressed every one of those limits.

"Cress, dear, I would like you to meet—"

"No!"

"I beg your pardon?" Amaryllis, having glanced toward the man who accompanied her, looked stunned.

"Whoever the gentleman may be with whom you have come here, I have no wish to meet him while you are attaching yourself to him."

"But you don't understand, Cress. It is extremely important—"

"Not to me." She didn't think that she had ever before interrupted somebody in mid-sentence, certainly not more than once. "I have spoken my last word on this subject."

Pointedly, she turned back to her previous vantage. The clubhouse that held Jemmy Dunster inside its limits seemed to be shimmering in the warm sun. By dint of concentration she identified a cluster of floribunda roses nearby and noted that they were hedged in by encroaching berberis. Her heart was hammering in part because of anger held in check.

"You must speak to her," Amaryllis was saying urgently, no doubt to the man at her side.

"The time is not favorable," he responded.

This brief conversation was enough to rouse Cressida's curiosity. It seemed as if the man was the one who wanted to communicate. In that case, Amaryllis's behavior might not have been objectionable.

It would behoove Cressida to find out the truth. When she looked around to begin doing so, however, she saw that the man and Amaryllis were walking off and out of earshot.

The answer to that riddle would have to wait. She had no intention of leaving the place into which she had maneuvered herself. With a shrug, she turned back to inspect the position of the clubhouse door.

And saw that it was opening.

Her resolve earned an immediate reward. Jemmy Dunster appeared, smiling. He was dressed acceptably in a yellow waistcoat, lined shirt, narrow trousers. Brown boots gave a discordant note to the ensemble, but anyone would understand the necessity for him to wear them at a racecourse. He was a gentleman to the shoe soles, was Lord Dunster.

Cressida leaned over and called his last name.

It had to be done twice again before he looked up, a hard hand shading his eyes. He smiled and raised a forefinger to indicate that she should stay in place. He was about to join her.

Briskly he spoke to the man who had walked out at his side. This latter looked up, too. At sight of the other, Cressida experienced a moment's panic. For it was this one, a frail-looking young fellow with bad posture and a Salvation Army righteousness, who had heard her telling mama that Jemmy Dunster was a damned fool. He would certainly repeat that tasty morsel of anecdote to his lordship if that hadn't already been accomplished. It seemed more than probable that he would gleefully identify the speaker.

If courtship could be compared to a horse race, Cressida found herself thinking, it might be that the greatest weights burdened only the strongest contenders.

CHAPTER FOURTEEN

"How good it is to see you again." Jemmy Dunster was smiling warmly.

She returned it, pleasurably noting once more the leathery outdoor-roughened skin and the light gray eyes with irises almost the same color. He may have thought he was being silently denigrated, because he tried to settle his broad shoulders more firmly into the waistcoat.

From his right came the sound of throat-clearing. His lordship's friend was waiting impatiently to be introduced.

"Oh yes, to be sure! This is my friend Osgood Nisbet. He's an M.P., and an Honorable as well, the latter only in title and not in his character."

"You mustn't take Dunster with too much seriousness," said the Honorable, adding a pallid smile, which suited his decayed appearance. "He is occasionally given to pleasantries of an odd type, I fear. I am indeed happy to make your acquaintance, Miss—"

Cressida gave her name and added a formal inquiry about how he did.

Almost as soon as he heard her voice, Nisbet's lips contracted sternly.

"I have heard that voice in the past, and now I think of it I have seen you as well."

"How pleasant for you."

"You are the gal who was speaking to an older woman at Cheshire and you called Jemmy a damn fool. I remember thinking at the time that it is unusual for anyone to assess him in that manner."

Cressida would not deny truth, as ever, nor make an apology.

If an oath had been hurled at Dunster in his presence, the peer would have risen to the challenge with blood in his eyes. This time, he did nothing more than shrug those strong shoulders.

"If Miss Cressida called me a name, then the possibility exists that at a certain time my conduct was such as to fully justify her."

The subject had been dismissed.

Cressida's eyes met his, each recollecting that sudden kiss. Her responses had fully equaled his. It must have surprised him as much as her.

In Cressida's imagination she could conceive a time when the two would be together. No matter how difficult a day both might have experienced, a touch of his hand would be enough to cause warm and avid responses in her.

Nisbet, seeing them engrossed, promptly excused himself. His half dozen words weren't heard. Sensibly he left without waiting for an acknowledgment, which would not be forthcoming.

Cressida wasn't aware of his departure. Although other strangers moved back and forth while holding conversations about very little, she felt as if the two of them were alone.

"We didn't get to discuss which horses you expect to furnish the victories for you today," she reminded him, thinking back to that recent charity affair at the Waghorn palazzo on Grosvenor Street. "I wonder if Lady Fortune is among them. She will be making an appearance in the second race, your first today."

"I am keenly anticipating excellent results from her, Miss Cressida. . . . I infer from your silence that you are not in agreement."

"Frankly, your lordship"—as though she could speak in any other manner!—"if I were writing Lady Fortune's condition book, I would say that for all practical purposes she is ridden out."

"Lady Fortune? Why, you can't have seen the Lady on any track."

"I certainly have, but I didn't know her owner at that time."

"Where did you see her?"

"Last year at Goodwood."

"That was a long race for her, Miss Cressida, and she does far better on the short variety. I wasn't aware of that at the time or I wouldn't have entered her."

"Were you aware how easily she can be distracted?"

"Certainly, but I couldn't help the rain during that race. I made urgent appeals for the rain to be halted, but they fell on deaf ears."

"And how often are you told about a good racing horse that can be put off by rain? Very seldom, I feel sure."

"I had never before seen her on a rainy track, Miss Cressida. I did know that she dislikes dust kicked back in her face, but that wasn't the problem I anticipated."

"She must be riding far behind to have that happen to her at all."

"Lady Fortune will be running with blinkers today to keep from being distracted."

"She is so easily rattled that she will be freshly distracted by the blinkers."

"How wonderful it must be to know everything."

"You will see, your lordship. It must follow that way, the horse being what she is."

"Lady Fortune's worst fault is that sometimes she cannot reach a smooth stride." Dunster was keeping his temper. "She is in good condition and an equable mood today and will win."

"My objection to the animal, fundamentally, is that she doesn't try hard enough."

"And I don't agree," Dunster said coolly. "In the words of some great sage, 'Differences of opinion make for horse races.'"

"I am betting on Quickstep for the second race, your lordship. If you wish to make an additional wager, a private one with me, I will cheerfully accept it."

"A private wager? Even if the prize is the same as last time?"

He was certainly referring to that kiss, which he had taken at Cheshire as the symbol of his victory.

"Let us repeat one condition of the first wager," said Cressida sunnily. "As before, the winner will determine the prize."

"Miss Cressida, you are a true sportswoman."

He glanced in the direction of the clubhouse door. Furrows suddenly ridged his forehead because of some unexpected sight.

"Regrettably, I must leave now. I hope to see you before this day is out so I may collect my winnings."

"And I, your lordship, feel exactly the same."

Dunster strode toward the stairs that would take him away from her. With one foot on the top step, he paused long enough to smile quickly and spare one wave of the right hand. Then he was gone. It was almost as if he had left for military service, considering the pangs she felt at his departure.

After the second race she would be returning to this exact spot. She would be found there by him. In the meantime, she had best return to her parents and impress them yet again by her willingness to be cooperative. Mama couldn't have been far away, but wasn't in sight at this moment, either. Cressida started toward the silver ring, where bookmakers were located. One relative or another must be looking at the boards with the names of horses and the odds being offered against their eventual victory.

She was halted by that young man with thick dark hair and brows, the one who had accompanied Amaryllis. He was by himself now, and planted firmly in front of her.

"You didn't want to talk to me before," he started.

"I feel the same about it now."

"I have to speak with you."

"I am sure it is important to you, for some reason. It is not important to me."

"For your own good, you must hear what I will say."

"Most likely this matter involves Amaryllis in some fashion. Are you going to transmit an apology from her?"

"Not at all."

Cressida's curiosity was sufficiently stirred for her to continue the talk.

"Then I don't know what you could possibly want. We hadn't met before a few minutes ago."

Kenneth Baldro was not celebrated for his humor, but he made a mildly droll observation now.

"I am offering you a chance to find that out."

"So you are, admittedly. Can this be accomplished soon?"

"If necessary."

"Can you convey your message or request or hymn—whatever it may be—without my having to leave this place?"

"Of course."

"Then if you will speak quietly, I think it is best for you to begin now."

CHAPTER FIFTEEN

Amaryllis had been left to her own devices by Mr. Baldro. It was unheard of that she should find herself in public without an elder to act as guide and shield. Given this current situation, everyone seemed a little different. As an unescorted female, she was drawing looks from males that could only be called speculative. As to the women, they were disapproving.

Her steps took her toward the crowded silver ring. Loudly dressed oddsmakers were dealing with bettors. If any male posed difficulties there, some other of the species would take her part. Common sense had its uses.

Straining her eyes in hopes of discovering a familiar face, she found Torin Fleet standing idly by. Her heart raced and she cared not at all that he was far from wealthy. Reliability was what mattered.

"I came with an acquaintance," she said swiftly after greetings had been exchanged. "The merest acquaintance. He has briefly left me alone."

Torin's firm blue eyes brightened upon seeing her, which was a comfort. Now he was looking down at a printed advertisement in a hand. His features had turned pensive.

"Whoever printed this must have been paid well for it and so was the person who thought of the sentiments contained here." The squib was an invitation to a temperance lecture that was going to be held nearby on the following evening. "The printers must do similar jobs."

Unlike Alice in the famous story by Mr. Lewis Carroll, she felt for a moment as if she had tumbled into the rabbit hole headfirst.

"Such people are able to earn an income, Amaryllis, and don't have to consider going to America or the South Seas, or joining Her Majesty's Army or Navy."

Not for the first time, her heart warmed to him. It did seem as if every feeling she had ever held about the lure of wealth had been tossed into the discard. Torin Fleet was responsible for that change. He had returned from the United States as a man in closer contact with reality, with everyday concerns. Whether that perception was correct or she was thinking in those terms so as to hide her own fascination with his maturing handsomeness, nothing could have been more likely than his recent statement to win warmth and fellow-feeling from Miss Wyse.

"Too many climates outside of England are difficult to live in," she said quietly. "A man's work must come first, but if that man were to marry while living elsewhere, his wife would have to bring up her daughters in, say, India. Raising one's children away from a first-hand appreciation of British traditions, I think, would be a sin."

"Marriage." Torin sounded wistful, as if he had thought of reaching for the moon. "How could a man in my straits consider marriage?"

"Such a man would be emboldened once he found a good woman who understood his feelings."

"Such a woman could not be found in Matabeleland, or wherever the winds of fortune might take a man who cannot do what is needed to help his wife and children take their proper place in society."

"Marriage is comforting and restful," she said, embarking on a pensée about the condition as such rather than talk about wives who were not British. "A participant doesn't always have to encounter new people and look upon each as if that person could change one's life."

"At risk of sounding like a heretic, I must say that I have enjoyed single blessedness. It is just that I feel a time coming when I will do so no longer."

"I believe the memory is soured when you realize that nobody has been close to you over the years, and as a result none knows you as having ever been young. To them, you were born old."

"As I interpret your view, it is that being married is only slightly better than the reverse."

"That is the grimmest possible way to look at it, Torin, but perhaps also the most practical. For some men and women marriage is better. For others, to be sure . . ."

"Your sudden reticence is understandable. A friend of mine found out early that his marriage was almost certain to be unsatisfactory. He had married somewhat beneath him and their first argument came when they woke up after the wedding night and he suggested that she ought to lend a hand getting breakfast together for them. The bride became angry and said, 'What kind of a woman do you think I am?' "

"In every sphere of life there are difficulties. No law says that a given marriage will be happy. One or the other might develop a loathing for the mate after only a brief time. With two people who know nothing about each other, that is entirely possible."

"I am inclined to feel that if I am not married by the time I reach ninety, I will yet be able to say that I am waiting for the most suitable of females to appear on the horizon."

Amaryllis was still taking the discussion seriously. "To marry is to gamble one's future on one's capacity to live productively with another human being. In all honesty I find myself thinking more and more that the gamble should be taken, and soon."

Had it been her own unwillingness to venture that had kept her so long from marriage? Or was it the need, unrecognized even by herself before very recently, to wait for the one certain man, the special man? Most importantly, had she discovered him to be someone she had known all these years?

Torin, for his part, was thinking along different lines.

"I could propose marriage today with some confidence of being accepted," he said huskily, matching her serious demeanor yet again.

"I—I feel sure that you could."

"But—"

He spoke no further. It had crossed his mind that he would need to inform Amaryllis about the family income being generated not by investments or inherited wealth. It was Cressida's ability to anticipate the performance of racing horses that made it possible for the Fleets to be accepted among the Sociables.

The revelation could have only one consequence. Amaryllis—darling Amaryllis—was certain to accept the news calmly and say nothing critical. But in her heart a wound would have opened, and it would fester. It would become impossible for her to be happily married into a family whose secret was one that she must shortly come to think of as odious.

Amaryllis, however, didn't know of any reason for the dismay in his eyes. She offered an encouraging smile and drew out a hand toward him.

Torin looked down at the soft gloved hand, plainly yearning to clasp it as some way of expressing the turmoil inside him. But he didn't touch her. It was as if he felt he didn't deserve even that much happiness.

"Please excuse me now," Amaryllis said, flushing hotly at what seemed like a slight. "I think I see my escort returning for me."

The flush remained as she walked off blindly, a haze before her eyes. Sudden pains streaked across her midsection and she was clutching at herself when she heard Mr. Kenneth Baldro speaking directly to her.

Amaryllis knew very well how to hide her own feelings while presenting an appearance of interest in the talk of another. With this particular matter, she did normally feel considerable interest. She started by forcing herself to listen to the alienist's first report, but soon found that every word of it was enthralling.

The second race began with that inevitable rush of horses past the gate. The animals' movements hardly exceeded Cressida's for quickness in returning to her favorite position. She took advantage of the opportunity to follow the race, well aware of the side view of the clubhouse. Jemmy Dunster would emerge from the front door not long after its conclusion, and would certainly be looking for her.

She was recovering from the recent conversation with Kenneth Baldro. It had been an unexpected diversion, on balance even a little unsettling.

Baldro had introduced himself as an alienist, a man whose vocation gave him an overwhelming interest in the mental illnesses of others. On occasion, this interest extended to mere foibles as well. Indeed a foible of hers had caused a good friend to arouse his professional instincts. This matter involved Cressida's future.

The serious-minded stranger launched himself into a description of the evils of betting on horses. That particular vice, to hear him tell it, had just about caused the destruction of Ancient Greece and the downfall of Ancient Rome. In Adam's fall, as he'd have said if he'd been blessed with the mother-wit to think of it, we wagered all.

It was the alienist's turn to be startled when he saw Cressida's family deferring to her in the matter of placing bets. Grimly he lectured Mama and then Papa (Torin seemed to be occupied elsewhere) about the wickedness of aiding someone with so dreadful an addiction. It would have been impossible to convince the flurried alienist of the truth about the family's income, even if such a course had been desirable.

"It is beyond current knowledge if such an obsession as yours can be treated with medication," the alienist had said when the bewildered elders left Cressida alone with him. "A rest cure could be beneficial, but I don't know of any location in the civilized world (by which, of course, I mean England) that is far away from the lure of the racing track and the turf accountant."

"That is probably so," Cressida agreed. She hardly knew what other contribution might be made to this lecture.

"I have a theory about such a difficulty," the alienist continued. "Indeed, my theory encompasses many mental foibles and reaches to identify their cause. Surely to know the cause is to be certain of a cure."

"Beyond any doubt."

She had been obsessed by nothing more than mild astonishment since the alienist's monologue began. It would have been child's play to speak several unmistakably direct words and turn away.

She was kept from such a course by the knowledge that it was Amaryllis who had unleashed Mr. Baldro. Amaryllis surely felt that she was acting in the best interests of a longtime friend (and prospective sister-in-law) in trying to help cure what she felt was a saddening condition. Like it or not, Cressida was powerfully moved.

"With enough of a sampling," the alienist continued, puffing himself up, "my theory might even gain a foothold of credibility in Vienna, the *fons et origo* of all decrees pertaining to my profession."

"Of course." One of the pleasanter aspects of dealing with him was that he made it easy to hide bewilderment or any reaction at all. It seemed like a curious trait in one who was concerned with the vagaries of the human mind.

"But we can discuss the application of my theory when you come for your first visit."

"My . . . first . . . ?"

"To my office in Harley Street. I am sure that Miss Wyse will accompany you, if you wish. Shall I expect you on Tuesday at eleven in the morning?"

"Yes. Yes, you'll expect me then."

Having determined not to be difficult at this time, she was nodding seriously. Before eleven o'clock on Tuesday morning Amaryllis would be told that the less of Mr. Baldro's company Cressida endured, the more chances existed for her disposition to remain sunny.

"In the meantime, Miss Fleet, if you must wager before your first session in my office, make the wagers very small."

"Indeed I shall. And now if you will be so kind as to pardon me, I will leave you."

The second race, the race in which she had made a bet with Dunster and against his entry, was getting under way.

CHAPTER SIXTEEN

Quickstep, the horse on which Cressida had advised the family to bet, turned out to be a fine choice. From the start, she ran to win. She made racing room for herself, so she certainly gained her reward by feeling like the monarch of all she surveyed. The jockey worked intelligently, preferring not to be showy rather than possibly impede his animal's great effectiveness.

Several of the jockeys on losing horses deserved praise for sparing the whip in their difficult situation. It was impossible to watch three of those riders without making a mental note to consider them as assets on any worthy horse they rode in the future.

Dunster's animal did not perform well. Lady Fortune started badly by veering from side to side in a waste of strength. At one point she appeared to hesitate, as if she had forgotten something. She did move at a reasonable speed for the last seconds of the race, but those splendid efforts ensured only that she would come in next to last.

There was a round of well-deserved applause for the winner. Cressida, watching silently, was pleased by her own skill in choosing the horse as an object of family wagering. Unless she was mistaken, at least twenty pounds could be considered the beginning of this day's earnings, this day's booty.

A brief wait ensued before Jemmy Dunster walked disconsolately out of the clubhouse. He moved between rows of sun-drenched magnolia, soulangeana, and grandiflora bordered by simple Kent cobs that seemed to be stooping sadly in mourning with him.

Cressida waved as he looked up and nodded slowly. He was prepared to endure the sort of deflation to which he had briefly exposed her before that fabled kiss had changed forever the way that Cressida would look at her future.

She was aware of what felt like a bone in her throat as she waited. Breath came with difficulty, and her back felt as if it was being repeatedly struck. Not until she called out did she realize she was giving a schoolgirlish squeal of anticipation.

His lordship was smiling again as he appeared at the top of the dark-painted stairs and took the first of several strides in her direction. He must have decided to pretend he wasn't unsettled by the results of the second race. There was almost a twinkle in those light gray eyes.

"Lady Fortune lost, as you surely know," he said in that baritone that was so sturdy and melodious. "You are at perfect liberty to refuse any dance with me from now on and not be a social outcast, as when you refused Wales not long ago."

Cressida was in no mood for persiflage. "What went wrong out there?"

"It was as you expected," he had to admit, still trying to sound cock-a-hoop, as if a substantial victory had been won. "She didn't take kindly to being blinkered so as to look only ahead. She started moving from side to side to get the blinkers off, then shaking her head for the same reason. You must have observed that."

"I assume she had behaved better at trials with blinkers on."

"Much better, but then, of course, there wasn't a field of horses or a horde of spectators to seem unnerving."

"Or to keep her from running as a horse must do if she has a competitive sense."

"You surely saw that she ran well toward the end."

"If there was a prize for the horse who runs best in the last seconds of a race, I feel certain that Lady Fortune would have gained a glorious victory. Unfortunately, however, that is not the criterion by which her performance has to be judged."

"I understand that, as you also predicted, Quickstep did win."

He must have known which horse had been triumphant. His pose was of an uncaring lack of knowledge on top of a fraudulent air of confidence. It was enough to convince Cressida that the ways of gentlemen simply surpassed all understanding.

"Quickstep didn't ride as if she was out for an airing on a

beautiful afternoon, my lord. From the minute she left the gate she was riding to win."

"Frankly I would have sworn that Lady Fortune would habitually perform better than she did today. That, however, is a common fallacy among those who fall short of victory on the racing course. I can but hope that a young lady like yourself, percipient as well as wealthy, has won more of the necessary to add to your already ample reserves."

She could not avoid looking upset at his continuing assumption that she was a person of prodigious wealth. It was one assumption that she could not dissipate until their relations were on a far better and more confidential footing. That prospect appeared to be rapidly receding into the distance.

"I admit that your prediction about the second race was entirely correct and I heartily congratulate you. Now if you will pardon me, Miss Cressida, I must bid you a reluctant adieu."

"No!"

"I—beg your pardon?"

"Granted."

"Thank you. As I said, I must leave."

"You have forgotten the wager between us."

"Oh yes, yes, of course, Miss Cressida. What a splendid thing that you've reminded me!"

"Not at all."

"It had very nearly slid out of my mind as these matters occasionally do."

"It wouldn't leave the mind of a winner."

"Miss Cressida, can we not postpone the reckoning on this matter? I am due to give final instructions to the young man who will be riding Varlet in the fourth race. I cannot therefore afford to spend much more time in your company at this juncture, relish it though I do."

"I thank you, your lordship, for those noble (so to speak) sentiments. It will need only another minute for you to pay your penalty, which, you will doubtless remember, I am to set."

"Very well, then. Very well."

"So we are therefore in agreement," Cressida said. "Please turn around, your lordship."

"I—what was that?"

"Please turn around."

"Might I ask why?"

"Of course you can ask."

In the absence of clarification, the peer shrugged and turned.

"I can only hope that this will not take too much time, as I have explained I must make an appearance at the paddock in order to—"

He broke off abruptly. Cressida had raised herself and leaned over. At a point just below his right ear, she kissed him.

She hadn't known she was going to do so. The impulse had come to her and been immediately acted on. At the touch of her lips on his skin, the closeness to him, she felt as if she was about to burst into several hundred sections.

There was a gasp of astonishment from a passerby who had turned around, jaw sagging.

In spite of his previously expressed rush to be gone, Jemmy Dunster did not move until his skin had been parted from her lips.

She was aware of probing gray eyes on her face and she felt excitement that wasn't like any she had known before, not ever. Not even when he had so impulsively kissed her.

"We shall see each other again," said his lordship decisively. "Count on it."

He ran to the stairs and was shortly lost to view. Cressida, having looked after him, felt that she had already done a good day's work.

For Jeremy Dunster, the carriage ride back to his home in Shropshire was an extraordinary occasion. He gave little thought to future plans for the unreliable Lady Fortune. Even less did he brood about Varlet finishing last. Most surprisingly, to anyone who knew him at all well, he spared not the slightest congratulations to himself over the two horses who had won.

His mind was on Miss Cressida Fleet.

He had sought her out after each race, but discovered her always in the presence of others. Parents, most likely. She seemed tense and withdrawn, not in the cast of mind to welcome an interruption.

He decided to seek her out as soon as he returned to London.

A letter would serve as a notification of intent. It seemed hideously abrupt to use the telephone for such a purpose. Besides, there was no certainty that her elders were listed on the phone and he would waste time finding out. Waiting to see her at another race meeting would need more patience than had been allotted to him for his time on earth.

He didn't suppose that her family would be most pleased by Jemmy Dunster as a companion for Cressida. Most likely it was his need to train and race horses that was certain to antagonize the wealthy Fleet family.

Dunster had never known a girl like Cressida Fleet. To some she might seem forward, to him she was blessedly direct. A man would always know her mood. None could imagine Miss Fleet acting stealthily.

Jemmy Dunster was not a stranger to the charms of the fair sex. He had attended young women who insisted that their escort be superbly dressed as well as anointed. The women were prepared to flirt and engage in the most inconsequential of discussions. He was not impressed by the company of these ladies. It was like trying to spend a social evening with a soufflé.

Cressida Fleet was blessedly different. She shared his interest in the improvement of the breed. In this area she was intuitively shrewd. She was in no fear of demonstrating wit and intelligence. With such a one a man could live the best times of his life.

It was a young peer in the grip of many emotions, therefore, who returned to Shropshire on Monday afternoon.

Just beyond the village of Little Pilkington he paused belatedly to check out the condition of his horses in the accompanying caravan. None was especially happy at the trip with the exception of the unpredictable Lady Fortune, whose stomach was as calm as a pond on a shiny day. Some financial arrangements would shortly have to be made about that steed for which he'd had such great hopes, Dunster told himself reluctantly.

He arrived at the main house of his estate in midafternoon, with the sun at its highest. He promptly supervised the stable lads in setting down the horses, then strode past the northern garden, where apple trees formed a boundary for the herbaceous borders. Those brilliant colors of lupin and delphinium, peonies, poppies, and day lilies, often caused him to smile. On this occasion he didn't give them so much as a glance.

He was welcomed by the butler. Crouch's square-rimmed glasses were foggy, as almost always, but that didn't keep him from immediately recognizing the master.

"The post is in your study, your lordship," he said after hearing about the racing results and explaining that very few calamities had taken place on the estate during his lordship's absence. "Sir Anthony has rung through on the telephone and asked you to return the call at your earliest convenience."

Dunster was issuing terse instructions soon after he stepped out of the telephone closet. Fresh clothing was to be packed for him instantly, enough to last until Friday. He would be going up alone to London, and the second carriage was to be ready to bring him to the train station at Little Pilkington.

To deal with the most urgent of matters during his absence, Dunster issued an additional order. Crouch was to to be in telephone communication with him at 6 P.M. every night, calling to the Albany in London. If his lordship should be unavailable, a message was to be left. His lordship wanted to know in detail what work had been done with each horse during every day of his absence, and whether changes had taken place in the condition of any of them.

He did not need to say that legislative matters in the House of Lords had reached a crisis, and that his presence was demanded for a crucial debate to be followed by a vote. Nearly all of his time and energies would be taken up for the next two or three days. He didn't expect that he would be able to collect his thoughts long enough to write a letter, not even a letter to the adorable Miss Cressida Fleet.

CHAPTER SEVENTEEN

Cressida was in a state of exaltation until she returned home to Albemarle Street. Her feeling had had nothing to do with the knowledge that the family was richer by sixty pounds because of her perceptions about the winning ways of certain horses. She remained stirred by the fact that she and Jemmy Dunster definitely possessed strong feelings about each other.

She was moved, too, by the conviction that luck had played into her hands in one respect. She'd told the family well in advance which horse she favored for the third race. Otherwise, Mama might have returned to seek her out and discovered at close hand that Cressida was briefly having her way with his lordship.

Happy though she was, and with excellent reason, a question came to mind. Not a doubt, certainly, but a puzzle that she couldn't resolve by herself.

She regretted not being able to confide in Mama, who spoke approvingly of marriage for an attractive daughter, but clearly saw such an event as causing the family income to vanish. Cressida didn't give a moment's thought to discussing this matter with Papa, who would puff at a cigar as he listened and not bring himself to question any remark from the family's money-maker.

Speaking to Amaryllis would gain nothing. Miss Wyse apparently felt that the act of wagering, even with success, was the devil's work. A possible marriage to some horse trainer, even if he was a peer, could not but speed the path of her destruction.

Only one likely confidant existed. She asked Torin to join her in the study.

Torin was in a difficult mood himself. It had been borne in on him after Kent that between him and the lovely Amaryllis there existed a barrier. This was caused, as he saw it, by his sister's occult affinity for choosing horses that won on the racecourse. Cressida, this sister of whom he was so fond, was keeping the family together and keeping him a dependent with a secret he couldn't divulge.

"Why didn't Jemmy Dunster come over to me afterward?" Cressida asked, having detailed the events that had involved her. "He could have come to see me after every race."

Torin knew that his sister had been looking like a thundercloud during the time to which she referred. He could now guess the reason. She had chafed at not being able to spend the day with the man of her choice, but had to occupy herself in other pursuits. As she made no secret of her unhappiness, any man would have hesitated to approach a female whose appearance would not have been substantially different if one of the track horses had stepped on her toes.

He would've explained this at any other time, adding that his beloved sister was the world's greatest goose. Showing affection for Cressida, no matter how well-deserved, would have been difficult in his particular state of mind. He chose, instead, to be unsettling.

"Dunster was pained that you could have been so forward."

"He was pleased!" Cressida protested immediately.

"I don't think that any other girl in society ever performed so mischievous a trick upon him, or behaved in public so little like a lady. What he must think of you now, Cressy, I don't know."

The quickest remedy for this possible setback occurred to her as soon as she was left to herself. She would put through a call to him on the telephone. Just as she was on the point of leaving this room, she remembered that it was her impetuousness that may have caused the complication. This was a time for subtlety, for restraint.

She turned toward the satinwood writing desk in the northeast corner of the room and reached for a sheet of gray stationery. She would indite a letter.

She wasn't the most efficient of letter writers as she could never think what to say after the first sentence. Having explained that she hoped her behavior back at Kent hadn't been a source of embarrassment to him, she dipped her pen in the inkwell and considered.

It seemed no more than appropriate to add congratulations on his two winners. In another choice of words she conveyed sympathy on the performance of Varlet, who had come in at the tail end of a procession of losing horses.

I hope we shall meet for the racing at Bath during this next weekend, she added, picking every phrase as if it would be her last. She knew while writing that she would insist upon the family attending those races. How easy it was to shade the truth!

In her final paragraph she expressed the hope that the weather at Bath would be better than adequate. In conclusion she wished him well.

She signed the letter with a flourish, but read it with growing disapproval. Nothing in it bore the slightest relationship to what she wanted to write. She'd have liked to say that she lived in hopes of feeling the strength of his arms about her and the sultry pressure of his lips upon hers. What she had written instead contained not one word that she urgently needed to communicate. It was socially correct, in an approved fashion for females. A tissue of lies.

She sealed it and pasted one of the new dried-glue stamps on the addressed envelope.

Only then did she shake her head violently and tear the envelope with the letter into halves. Those halves were then shredded into quarters.

She decided against writing another cluster of insincerities. She would confront Jemmy Dunster at Bath and make certain that he hadn't been offended by a moment of lusty feeling expressed with honesty. The truth was mighty and it would prevail.

Mama had recently determined upon redecorating the second-floor rooms before the end of this social season. Perhaps in July.

Her home entertainment for this season would take the form of a reception early on the month following. For that August occasion she was planning to engage Signor Giuseppe Ortolozzi, now of Covent Garden, to give a recital upon that Bechstein piano, which Cressida had never learned to play. She would also engage some deep-voiced actor to offer a reading from the works of the late Mr. Dickens. The many guests would be able to sit in freshly decorated quarters after overeating at supper and feel sympathy with the sufferings of the poor.

Another improvement called for Papa to buy one of the new horseless carriages. Torin had spoken with approval of a model called the Wombat Runabout. Ownership of such a treasure would prove beyond peradventure of doubt that the Fleet family was in the social swim, was modern.

Money would have to be sequestered for these purchases. Gladys Fleet was far too practical to urge her nearest and dearest to earn more by betting a monkey, as a five hundred pound wager was called. Such an outlay might result in a painful loss. She felt the same about a pony bet, convinced that an adverse speculation of even twenty-five pounds on one bet was more than flesh and blood should have to endure.

She had temporized by instituting a string of economies. The quality of food had been substantially lowered. Three house maids had been given their *congé*. It might be possible to drop Mrs. Durbin, the housekeeper, to three workdays a week and pay accordingly.

Her most stringent economy was the insistence that no clothing be purchased, but that current possessions be altered when possible so as to seem new. Cressida wouldn't agree to such a regimen and risked maternal displeasure by making those few purchases she wanted. Torin had become disputatious over the new rule, spurred by an outbreak of deeper feelings and a desire to look splendid when in the company of Amaryllis. Papa, of course, went along without dispute.

Mama was continually setting the best example herself. On this Tuesday morning in her room, she had put on an old dress and was discussing changes that might lend it a fresh appearance.

Cressida and the seamstress had joined in the deliberations. It was pointed out by Cressida that the diagonal front drapery must remain, but that the crystal trim could be removed. As for the white French bunting, it could be given a different shape. A color change seemed suitable as well, turning it black.

"I hope not to look like an out-of-use electric bulb," Mama said, having confronted her imagination in the three-sided mirror. "How soon can the work be done, Mrs. Boggs?"

"This afternoon," the seamstress decided. "You'll look as good as spankin' new, ma'am, beggin' your pardon for the expression."

Into this vortex of decision-making, Mrs. Durbin, the square-faced housekeeper, ventured imperturbably.

"Miss Wyse to see you," she whispered to Cressida. "Says that the two of you had agreed to meet here and at this time."

A girl who was less well-bred might have sworn under her breath. Cressida had been occupied since yesterday dreaming while awake about the various good features of Lord Jeremy Dunster. In her free time she had prepared the family for its next outing at the racecourse in Bath. Small wonder she had neglected to let Amaryllis know that she didn't have the least intention of being interviewed by that strange and humorless man, Mr. Baldro.

If she was going to make her feelings entirely clear, there was no remaining time but the present.

In the downstairs drawing room, she discovered Amaryllis looking superb in a white day dress with black lacing at various significant points. She was radiant, a condition for which the rig-out was not entirely responsible.

Torin was in this same room and only three steps or so away from her. They might have pulled themselves apart with some suddenness, perhaps because of Cressida's footsteps on the stairs. Each was breathing, but only with the greatest difficulty. Neither was taking the trouble to glance away from the other.

"I am on my way to the study for some work," Cressida said, happy at the opportunity to be by herself.

"No!"

Amaryllis, galvanized, asked Torin to excuse them and to close the door as he left. Torin started to shake his head, but took the precaution of glancing from one young female to another. The drawing room door was closed forcefully with a sound that must have resembled a cannon shell being discharged in the heat of battle.

"Cress, I have come to take you for your first consultation with Mr. Baldro."

"Nonsense!"

"Do you mean that you decline to become a happier person?"

"That may be how you choose to think of it. There is a point to remember, however, to cherish, to keep in mind above all others on this issue. It is simply that under no circumstances whatever will I accompany you or anyone else to the chambers of that miserable man."

"In which case," said the lovely Amaryllis, drawing herself up, "I shall be forced to tell your mama that I saw you amorously attacking Jeremy Dunster at the racetrack in Kent."

Such a revelation would cause fresh-minted difficulties. Quarrels were more than likely to fill many an hour that ought to have been devoted to Cressida's systematic consideration of Jeremy Dunster's speech and appearance, not to mention the vivid recollection of his touch.

"I would be doing this," said Amaryllis self-righteously, "only to aid a good friend who is the plaything of a grievous affliction."

"I would rather you called a meeting of my worst enemies and sent them in to see me," Cressida said spiritedly.

"Nor do I deserve sarcasm from you."

On behalf of any cause that she felt was just, Cressida's dear friend could be a tartar. It was difficult to keep from feeling a moment's sympathy for Torin. One of his goals in life involved linking himself to a female whose single-mindedness made the late Inspector Javert seem like a flibbertigibbet.

"If my understanding of your position is correct," Cressida said briskly, searching for a *modus operandi* that would leave both of them mildly dissatisfied instead of causing one girl to go to some extreme, "you don't wish to set my mama against me."

"Not unless I am required to do so by the obligations of friendship."

"A discussion of the duties of friendship can be profitably postponed," Cressida said drily. "If your mind is not entirely dead to compromise, however, I am prepared to offer a suggestion."

Amaryllis was silent.

"On my part, the concession I make is in going to see this man today."

"Certainly."

"Wait! Having spoken with him, I then decide for myself whether or not I wish to see him again professionally."

"Now, Cress," her friend began.

"And it is understood that if I decide against returning to his chambers I shall not be pestered about it ever again."

"This is not fair!"

"I can make no better offer than that," Cressida pointed out. "Half a loaf for each is better than none."

"Mr. Baldro can accomplish nothing, I feel sure, with only a solitary meeting."

"It is possible, as he is so great a man to your way of thinking, that he can persuade me to see the error of my ways."

"In other words, Cress, you want me to take a gamble."

It was Cressida's turn to fall silent.

Slowly, slowly, Amaryllis nodded in acceptance of the terms.

CHAPTER EIGHTEEN

"Before you speak in any detail," said the great man, "I will ask you to lie down on this couch."

Cressida shook her head immediately. "Certainly not!"

"Your friend is in the waiting room. If anything untoward were to happen, she would hear your reaction to it."

"She is indeed there, but on the other side of the door. I am on this side."

Baldro's sharp features had changed in complexion from sturgeon gray to oyster white. He may have been outraged at the thought of anyone who considered that he would give in to an impulse.

"Good day," said Cressida, rising from her chair.

"If you wish, Miss Fleet, you may remain seated while we converse, but the results will not be as effective."

"I am prepared to chance that." Cressida marveled at herself. In spite of this man's provoking behavior, she sounded restrained.

The chambers did not look as if anyone in them had ever smiled, let alone laughed. In the keystone of a facing arch was the figured marble bust of a most unBritish-looking gentleman as solemn as Baldro himself. At least one of the chairs hadn't been designed for comfort. The shine of desk edges was enough to hurt the eyes. A sporting print was placed where it couldn't be seen by someone not looking for a painting. No, Baldro's idea of a relaxed evening probably consisted of reading a history of the gunpowder plot.

Cressida answered a host of queries about her recent wagering and that of various family members. She answered truthfully before it occurred to her that she might be revealing more than she wanted him to know. On second thought, however, she saw no possibility of Baldro being able to figure out as a result the dread secret of the Fleet family.

"Do you take much pleasure in the laying of these wagers?"

"Not particularly."

"Aha!" The alienist nodded two times where another man might have smiled. "In that case, I feel that something can be done to help. I am happy to tell you that such assistance as you need is not now beyond the limits of possibility."

Cressida saw no reason to feel gratified by this news. If she put herself in the alienist's hands, she and her family would be on their uppers by the end of June.

"Tell me something else, Miss Fleet, and much may depend on it. Do you have any recollection of what foods you were fed as a baby?"

If Cressida had made out a list of queries she might expect from this source, something along those lines would have come in dead last.

"Foods? Not in the slightest. Why should my years-ago regimen, whatever that may have been as far as comestibles might be concerned, remain of the slightest interest to anyone now?"

"Here, Miss Fleet, we are in uncharted waters. Let me briefly explain. The modern alienist in this year of 1897 stands on the threshold of vital discoveries about the agitations that misshape human lives."

Cressida supposed she was glad of that much.

"The Master of us all"—and he looked respectfully toward the figured marble bust of some bearded foreigner—"has indicated his belief that such difficulties could be caused by stimuli encountered in the first years or even months of life."

Never having given the least thought to the problem or its possible solution, Cressida was at a loss for any response that would be sincere.

"As a result, I have worked up a theory to clarify the conception. If my theory was to win acceptance in the hallowed offices of Vienna, my name would be enshrined in the history of this exalted vocation. Think of it, Miss Fleet! Freud, Breuer, Jones, and Baldro marching together shoulder to shoulder through the pages of history."

Cressida was unable to imagine four humans marching through volumes of whatever size. Once again, she took refuge in silence.

"Your malady, your fever, can offer evidence in support of my theory that the foods one is given in early life are determining factors in one's mental health afterwards. When I write my paper on the subject, your initials will have an honored place. 'At the time I was consulted by C.F.,' my paper will say, 'she was a haunted and haggard wretch who—' "

"I have heard enough," said Cressida, rising for the second time and with more determination.

The alienist was startled by a response so strongly against this young woman's best interests as he saw them. Miss Fleet wasn't a patient he would lose without making a great effort to keep her patronage. A patient who was one of the Sociables would facilitate his acceptance as an honorable practitioner of a difficult craft in its pioneering years.

Only as she started to the door did he speak those words that were most likely to cause Miss Fleet to pay attention. He would otherwise have thought them too frivolous.

"You came clearly distraught, and my help can give you peace of mind, which will be reflected in your appearance."

Cressida considered herself to be unsettled about Dunster, edgy over the future of her brother, and out of sorts with Miss Wyse. She did not until that moment think of herself as being distraught.

"I would certainly not come to this place and see you alone," she said without disguising that particular concern. "However, if we were to meet elsewhere, we could speak briefly."

"Some other place?" No similar suggestion had ever been heard in these precincts. "What, exactly, would you have in mind?"

"During the season I attend various functions, as you surely know."

She was abashed when the alienist suddenly flushed to the tips of his ears. It occurred to her belatedly that he might not be able to attend those occasions as he was unlikely to have been invited.

"But I do appear in public when I go to various racing courses."

"Let me see if I understand the full import of what you are communicating." The alienist had to pause now that he was aware of this young woman's breathtaking effrontery. "You propose that I attempt to keep you from wagering by speaking to you on the premises of any racing course you name. Is that correct?"

Cressida saw no reason to repeat herself.

It must be reported in all candor that Cressida was considering that the alienist might be of some use in a way which he didn't anticipate. If she was seen in conversation with a young man while at the racing course, Jemmy Dunster could feel an onset of jealousy. Such an emotion might cause him to accelerate his plans to take her hand in marriage.

Even to Cressida, it was not a strategem that reeked of subtlety. That special quality would have been irritating. No elegant and drawn-out courtship would be suitable, but would cause her to become furious. She wanted her own directness to be matched by his. A brisk announcement of their engagement would be followed as quickly as possible by the wedding. At St. Peter's in Eaton Square, if at all possible.

"I have every intention of attending the races at Bath this Saturday," she informed the alienist. "If you wish to speak with me when I am not otherwise occupied, please feel free to do so."

Baldro, aware of his own need for recognition from the Sociables and the affluence to be gained from their patronage, fell silent.

She turned without seeing the alienist's reaction. He wouldn't be proud of having to accede to a condition he viewed as being outrageous. Sparing his sensibilities gave him the opportunity to pretend later on that he had accidentally encountered her. Cressida Fleet's nature was not without a strong vein of generosity.

She was in a cheerful mood upon returning to Albemarle Street. It had already given her satisfaction to tell Amaryllis in all truth that she would be consulting Kenneth Baldro in the future. The carriage ride on this warm day had brought a different sort of pleasure. At her direction, the carriage detoured through Fleet Street. Plain folk were walking in a leisurely way from Temple Bar to Ludgate Circus, pausing to examine hoardings of news bulletins and discuss the contents with strangers. These comfortable people could have accepted the worst news, she thought optimistically.

Nor did she allow herself to become annoyed when she dressed for supper and the lace on her light blue bengaline gown developed a slight gash. She changed immediately to the clouded moiré. Silently she permitted one of the maids to make urgent repairs on her blond crown.

In front of the closed door to the dining room, however, her equanimity was tested. Papa was once again criticizing Torin.

"You should have attended Brasenose at Oxford, as I did," Papa was saying, an autocrat with his son in part because he couldn't rule over the women in his immediate family. "Perhaps you realize now that education can help any young man gain employment in business."

"I don't want to be in trade of that sort, guv'nor," Torin protested, not for the first time. "Why, a man in trade can be dismissed at the whim of anyone who is possessed of greater wealth. He is playing cards with no idea of what the game might be."

"Bosh *and* tosh!" Papa snorted. "You want to be in charge of an enterprise, but can't accept the simple fact that I am unable to pay for you to embark on such a folly."

"I am sorry that you don't approve of my ambitions, guv'nor."

"They are schemes that have no chance of working out. If I had the ready, I would purchase a commission for you in the Queen's forces."

Torin laughed without mirth. Whenever he talked about politics, he opposed the excesses of British colonialism. Since coming back from America he loudly applauded the spirit of the Yankees in setting themselves free of what he called the British yoke. The lion's tail, he liked to say, ought to be more frequently twisted. He favored politicians who spoke about the need to forego empire building and look to home interests. It did seem as if he had made it a point to find out which opinions would most offend his parents and promptly acquire them.

Pacifically taking her husband's side, Mama told him, "You have to be understanding, dear, as well as patient with the foibles of the young."

Papa subsided, but kept muttering. It would have been clear to the smallest intelligence that the self-appointed lord of the manor was dissatisfied with his son.

It was time for Cressida to make a contribution. "When it is at all possible, I would hope that you and Mama could withhold adverse judgments until the last possible moment."

Papa stopped muttering because of implied censure from the family member who performed that vital function which was beyond his capacities. He was reduced to glaring at his son.

Mama caused a distraction by telling the housekeeper to convey compliments to Mrs. Fawthorp, the cook. That good Scottish lady had introduced a side dish of carrots with adhering ginger. The combination, which at first bite ought to have caused the palate to wither, became endurable and then pleasant. As often happened with Mrs. Fawthorp, the additional foods were prepared impeccably. The fish or meat entrée, in this case broiled cutlets *soubise,* could have used some improvement.

During the interval, Torin had gathered his forces together to change the original subject and make a happier contribution.

"I think I have *some* good news," he began, with a meaningful look at his sister.

Only his earnestness kept Cressida from making a wry rejoinder. He had inherited the prominent Castle family chin from Mama and it gave him a look of nose-to-the-grindstone pertinacity. He wasn't afraid to put himself forward when he knew he was right. In that way (and some others), Cressida often considered him an admirable brother.

"What would that be?" she asked.

Papa, aware of her sudden interest, feigned or not, transferred his glare to the unoffending carrots. He was obviously prepared to criticize once again if anyone should be dissatisfied with the contents of Torin's news.

"You know Dickon Daymore, of course. Well, he got it into his head that we must see a session of the Lords today. They were taking up a measure to do with sporting events, and Dickie is a member of the Torbay Yacht Club in Torquay."

Cressida wanted to ask urgently whether Torin had seen that one certain peer who was of such great interest to her. This wasn't the place or time for that question. She wished she had been free long enough for him to have offered a full account earlier and in privacy.

"Nearly all of the first hour was taken up by a matter of procedure. It was necessary to admit Hubert Quixwood, who has become Lord Enham now that his guv'nor handed in his club memberships, so to speak. You know of that, of course. Well, Hubert entered, looking as if he had just been stuffed and mounted on one of his guv'nor's walls. Two peers dressed in fiery red accompanied him. Then Hubert made his bow to the Lord Chancellor who was, bless us all, on the woolsack for this monumental occasion. The writ of summons was read and the oath administered. Then he was led to his seat by the Garter-King-at-Arms in his tabard, no less. The writ was then received by the clerk of the house. But the exercise had not yet been completed. Hubert then rose from his seat and returned to the Lord Chancellor, who congratulated him upon becoming a member of the house of peers. It was difficult, I can assure you, not to doze through any of this."

Cressida's patience was under a severe strain. "Will you please tell me—tell us—what news of importance you bring?"

"I am coming to it immediately," he said, before that dormant volcano who was his own guv'nor once more became active. "Dickie knows virtually the entire strength of the company, so we went out to join some members for dinner. It was time for an intermission in the day's theatrical endeavors."

Papa asked irritably, "Are you going to tell us that you have learned more in your life than some French and some mathematics and some Bible studies? If so, I wish you would offer proof of it."

Torin overlooked this incitement to continue the recent quarrel. "One of the peers to whom I was introduced told me that he has met you. He is a horse owner and his name, as nearly as I can recall, is Dunwoody."

It was easy to guess what must've actually happened. Torin would have been eager to meet Lord Dunster and judge for himself the strength of any possible attachment between the peer and Cressida. No doubt Torin hoped to see his sister happily married. Such an arrangement, as he very well knew, would leave him in the position of being the family money-earner. If he never published a racing paper, as he hoped to do, he could certainly muster additional skill to forecast satisfactorily which racing horses would be most likely to win at particular sporting events.

"The name is not Dunwoodie," Papa snapped, surprisingly. "It is Dunster."

"I think you're right, guv'nor."

"I *know* I am." More mildly, even reflectively, Papa added, "I knew his father. I do believe that on various and sundry occasions I danced with the girl who became his mother. Both are now deceased, I am sorry to say. Or as you, Torin, would put it, they handed in their club memberships."

"Dunster told me that he hopes to see you in Bath over the weekend, Cressida, and to make the acquaintance of our elders, as he put it."

Cressida smiled down at her tea.

Papa began, "Do you have anything more to tell—?"

He was interrupted firmly.

"I doubt if any of us has a statement of real importance to make, Mr. Fleet," said Mama with iron courtesy. "And as the meal is concluded, let us resume our placid lives."

Papa would show not the least anger toward his son as they sat alone at table long enough for him to smoke one cigar before both rose to join the ladies.

Cressida gave some brief consideration to pleading weariness and retiring early. That way, she wouldn't hear speeches about the necessity to postpone possible marriage. If Mama was going to speak critically, let it be done as soon as possible. And let the answer be made immediately.

No sooner had she occupied the simple Eastlake chair in the upper drawing room than she brought up the subject.

"I suppose you are wondering about Jemmy Dunster and my feelings toward him."

"I am sure you realize the family's position and our reason for it," Mama said, dislodging a furniture-top ornament that had found its way to the cushion of her favorite mahogany Burmese chair.

Cressida refrained from snapping that such a remark was not entirely responsive. "It should be enough to tell you that if I can persuade him to marry me, I shall certainly do so."

"You intend to persuade him without the use of physical violence, I hope, Cressy. As you are a member of the so-called gentler sex, it would be inappropriate to hold both hands around his neck, say, and threaten to squeeze the breath out of him until he consents to your proposal."

"I didn't intend to provide amusement," Cressida said stiffly.

Mama had the grace to flush.

"You want to know my feeling, do you? I would be opposed to such a union only for reasons that have to do with the family's welfare, as I indicated just before. There has been no change in my feelings during the last moments."

"I must point out that my brother is of an age to carry the burden of supporting both of you as soon as such a need might arise."

"Certainly, but his ability to prognosticate the outcomes of races has not been nearly equal to yours."

"He could improve his skills, much as I have done."

"If he cared to, I feel sure he could. But his goal in life is to be wholly unfettered, to do exactly what he wishes. Such a path is not compatible with the duty of maintaining his elders in the comfort that they surely deserve as they move uncertainly toward decay and the grave."

"I rather feel that Torin may in the future be more amenable to such duties."

"Might I ask why?"

"Torin has found a heart interest."

"The mother is always last to know," said Mrs. Fleet drily. "Does she feel the same way about him?"

"I am certain that she does."

"And may I now ask the name of this excessively fortunate member of our sex?"

"I refer to Amaryllis Wyse."

"So? I would not have thought that she, of all your friends, would be pleased at the state of Torin's finances."

"That is almost certainly so, but she apparently feels that Torin is a better man since he returned from his voyage to Yankeeland."

"Is that enough to explain the sudden transformation of her character?"

"I am sure I need not add, Mama, that the heart has its reasons."

"With Amaryllis Wyse, I would have said that the purse has its reasons," Mrs. Fleet said tartly.

"My point is that these developments will cause Torin to be more susceptible to to the idea of earning an income by some mode not previously seen by him to be an ideal one."

"Possibly." Mama's lips thinned uncertainly at first. At an afterthought, they thinned even more in disapproval. "And I must tell you that I am not made deliriously happy by the prospect that the Wyse family may soon be *au courant* of the family's position in society and how it is maintained. Lady Beryl is a notorious gossip and mightn't be deterred even if we became family connections."

There was a pause. Cressida's mind returned immediately to the major difficulty under discussion.

"But you want me to cease immediately to have anything to do with Jemmy Dunster. Is that correct?"

Glady's Fleet's sharp eyes probed at her daughter. When she looked away, she might have been speaking to herself.

"I was conversing a minute ago about decay and the grave, which may be not to the point at this moment. It occurs to me that in transit to dissolution a woman's opinions and feelings undergo alteration."

Cressida realized that Mama's tone of voice had been modified to one of reflection. Silently she waited to hear more.

"A young woman thinks that love means possession, Cressy. She possesses a dog or a cat and it is forced to stay close to her. Therefore it loves her. To a young woman, too, parents are an eternal possession."

"And later on, what of a husband?"

"Similarly, husband and wife begin their true closeness under the same roof. Love is symbolized by that closeness. Time advances and a husband may pass away first. It is not that the love has diminished, but that the years have compelled change that cannot be controlled by either participant."

"Are you now about to tell me that the same situation applies between elders and children?"

"Indeed it does, Cressy. A child may not love its elders any the less, but in a different way than before as time advances. The child wants to make a change that will take him or her away from the house where the elders have been given love and where it has been loved in return. Of necessity the elders must realize that to love a descendant may sometimes mean to give freedom to her or him, to let the descendant leave. One has to allow the young to change when the time seems right. To be a mother is to watch someone alter from baby to child to youth and then to an adult who wants to marry and go elsewhere. In one form or another, the love of elder for descendant is a process of continuous leavetaking."

Cressida was moved to rush over to Mama and enfold her in a warm embrace. The Fleet females held on to each other and cried softly.

They were professing their love for each other when the door opened on Papa and Torin, who had come to join them for a family evening.

CHAPTER NINETEEN

Cressida hadn't expected an overlong carriage ride to Bath, but luck was against her. Repairs had to be made at a wheelwright's near the high plains of Gloucestershire. At Chippenham, the horses had to be watered.

She felt as if she had been waiting a long time to renew her acquaintance with Jemmy. She felt as if she and the family had been traveling to Bath since the dissolution of the monasteries in the year 1593. It can truthfully be said that Miss Fleet was not in the best possible humor.

Mama, on the contrary, seemed entirely at ease. She had occupied most of the trip in lecturing Torin. His forthcoming marriage to the wealthy Miss Wyse, if indeed it took place, was now seen by her as possibly giving the family access to a more dependable income than had previously been their lot in life.

"You have the intelligence, my dear Torin, to make strides when everyone else is rooted to one place. You have the capacity to make firm decisions and to execute them."

Torin had been surprised at first to hear himself so well spoken of. He soon recalled that Cressida had notified him of such a turnabout possibly taking place before many more sunsets.

Papa listened open-eyed to this description of a son who had previously been alien to him. He did not speak his disagreement, but sat with reading spectacles held in one hand by the stems. He looked like an older butler astonished by the package that had been given to him on Boxing Day.

"To gain even greater assurance, my dear Torin, I feel that you should spend as much of the day as possible in the company of your sister. You can observe how and why she moves in mysterious ways her wonders to perform."

The words were spoken lightly but they gave Torin a spasm of jealousy because of the clear inference that his prowess was not yet on a level with his sister's. As for Cressida, the prospect of being in Torin's presence while she spoke with Jemmy was enough to worsen her mood even further, a feat which she would not have thought was possible.

Daymore, the coachman, took them into the celebrated village of Bath by way of Sion Hill. He approached Lansdown Crescent like a warrior sighting some enemy. As a result of his dillydallying, none of the family noted the classically lovely view of splendid buildings on what looked like slightly tilted streets.

There was no immediate sign of Jemmy when the spacious and comfortable course was finally reached. He must have been occupied by the two horses he would be racing. One of these was Varlet, whose chances she didn't favor. The horse came in fourth, but better luck might have given him a second. It was a far better showing than Cressida would have anticipated for him.

Jemmy didn't make an appearance in the spectator area after Varlet's race. Perhaps the steed had been afflicted in some way and immediate care was necessary. She would be ill-tempered indeed not to give him the benefit of every possible doubt.

Kenneth Baldro, however, was standing close by and waiting for Torin to be sent away before he could be ostensibly consulted and actually be seen in her company. Cressida did send her brother off, but only because it would be easier to devote herself to looking around for Jemmy.

The alienist approached respectfully. He was dressed with severity, which was no source of astonishment.

"Have you placed a wager on the forthcoming contest, Miss Fleet?" he began in the sort of tone with which a physician might have inquired about signs of leprosy.

"My family has done so."

"I—yes, I should have expected as much. Frankly, Miss Fleet, I have been in detailed conferences with my peers. The telephone has been useful in this endeavor, as you may imagine. These extraordinary circumstances have led me and a colleague who shall be nameless to formulate an experimental course of treatment for your unfortunate obsession."

Cressida had mistaken a vigorous spectator at a distance for

Jemmy. As a result she lost immediate interest in the alienist's prattling.

"I must now put a crucial question." Baldro turned first, so that he could be identified by a patient, the fifth Baron Allingham. The Fifth baron merely shrugged at the sight before him and moved off. "Do you plan to bet on every race?"

Cressida heard the question three times before realizing that it was directed at her.

"All but the third," she said. "That one is a battle of mediocre animals, and I see no likely profit to speculating on its outcome."

"So there is one race upon which you are not making a bet." Baldro rubbed his hands, which were surprisingly large and rough for a man who worked with intellect. "You are not wholly enslaved to the demon of wagering. Excellent, excellent!"

"No, merely practical," Cressida pointed out with a dry bluntness that would have won admiration from Mr. Holmes of Baker Street.

"Here is what you are to do, then, Miss Fleet. This time you are wagering on the outcome of eight races and cannot be dissuaded with words. So be it. Next time you attend a race meeting, you must only wager on seven of the races."

"What?" Cressida's attention was very nearly caught. "You undertake to cure me of betting by insisting that I continue to do so?"

"And the time after that, you are to bet on six races only. After that, five. Then four. Do you understand now what I urge you to do?"

"I understand your words, yes, but not the thinking behind them. If you attempted to cure me of too great a consumption of alcohol, such advice would result in my being put into a charity hospital ward posthaste."

"Miss Fleet, this advice has been conceived by one of the finest minds in Vienna."

"Not that it matters," Cressida murmured, dismissing the end product of Viennese thought. It seemed as useful as some of the pastries that had been conceived in that location.

"But Miss Fleet, you must believe in the bona fides of the colleagues with whom I have consulted."

There was nothing to say in response. Following the recent example of the fifth Baron Allingham, she walked off.

From a distance, his voice raised, Baldro called, "We must endure a hiatus, now."

Cressida had never heard a more inappropriate sentiment expressed so foolishly.

She had seen Torin and the family in conversation with another man. This one looked around avidly even while responding to whatever observations were made to him. That stranger was very special.

His eyes caught sight of her and seemed fixed as she moved in his direction. He gave off a belief in his own strength rather than the indecision that had afflicted other males in contact with her. This one looked at her as if he knew that her warm flesh would be giving in this place and firm in that. As if he wanted nothing more than to offer the greatest happiness with a man that would ever be hers.

Little wonder that her knees felt weak. She gave no thought to the lying of that silver-gray vigogne cloak, which Mama once insisted that she purchase, or the bonnet that strategically allowed half a dozen tendrils of shiny blond hair to peep out. Nor did she give the least consideration to subduing the eagerness with which she ran to him.

Mama's voice, as if from a distance, was saying, "Cressy, you must recall Lord Dunster. Lord Jeremy Dunster."

"To be sure."

"His lordship has made a suggestion that you, too, will find of interest," Mama continued, the volume of her voice receding as Cressida continued to inspect his lordship. "Despite the demands of the social season in London, Lord Dunster suggests that it might be of interest to us all to visit him midweek at his estate in Shropshire."

Cressida's heart gave such a leap that it bade fair to fall out from between her lips.

"It offers a chance to show you my horses, as you are all such great patrons of the sport of royalty." Jemmy had eyes for no one but her. "You will be able to see and appreciate the caliber of work that is involved in their training."

"I hope that my elders will consent to so useful a visit."

"Further, I can happily renew my acquaintance with Mr. Torin. And with you, Miss Cressida."

Happily, indeed!

Cressida nodded, having briefly forgotten how to produce speech.

Papa certainly understood the sense of the meeting. He cleared his throat.

"We would be honored, your lordship, to accept so kind and thoughtful an invitation."

Cressida was suddenly possessed by the notion that if she exchanged glances with Dunster at this moment, the two of them would burst into the most unseemly laughter!

"I see only a solitary way to resolve the problem," Mama said carefully, with a sudden sideways look at her daughter.

They were in the upstairs drawing room. Mama was knitting while Cressida thought of Jemmy and wished she had seen more of him during the recent day. Or at least that they could have spoken together in privacy.

It was the sort of early June afternoon that passed for sunny by the usual standards of London. The family disposition matched this weather, the Fleets having returned from Bath richer by no more than thirty pounds. Jemmy's second horse had not justified the confidence shown by Cressida. Profits for the weekend, as a result, hadn't been exceptional. They'd been no more than barely reasonable.

"To what problem do you refer?" Cressida asked, forcing her mind to the subject that Mama had just brought up.

"It is quite simple, Cress. I can not be certain how good a catch Lord Dunster might be for you."

"An excellent—"

"Please! I know he has horses and an estate as well as a seat in Parliament. But the horses may be an expense that isn't earning him a serious income. As far as an estate is concerned, should farm crops pose difficulties there could be a wave of defaults, and the land will be no more a source of profit than last week's racing papers."

"One can be certain about very little in this world, judging from my small experience."

"Quite true, but I want to be convinced that he is intelligent enough to make some recovery of his fortunes in case circumstances suddenly become adverse."

"Do you anticipate being able to divine that much?"

"What I anticipate, Cressy, is to talk with someone who must have made an assessment of his lordship as she has done with every unmarried and eligible male in Britain."

Cressida's brows rose. "You don't mean Amaryllis?"

"I do indeed. If she has no opinion, then the truth, as dear Dr. Constable tells us on Sundays in another connection entirely, is unknowable by mere mortals."

"Do you plan to visit the Wyse home and speak to the Oracle?"

"I think that the information I seek can be conveyed on that barbarous instrument, the telephone."

"Very well, Mama. I will speak with Amaryllis immediately, if you wish."

"Greet her and then give me the—thing," Mama instructed. "You are too enthralled by circumstances to comprehend the full weight of every word."

Cressida didn't favor such unimpeded communication. Amaryllis had already expressed decided views against Dunster. The one hope that Cressida found herself feeling was caused by her friend having expressed strong views, too, against wagering. Both of these might be communicated, and the vehemence of the latter could very well cancel out any speculative views of the former.

Mama would not be balked in her purpose. Cressida approached the telephone closet as if it hid some viper. She caused delays in making contact with the connection, hoping that Mama might become impatient. The older woman gestured through the partly opened door for her to hurry. After more introductory words to her friend than were needed, she reluctantly stepped outside.

Mama began shouting from the moment she took Cressida's place, as if Amaryllis were several yards away and couldn't understand normal speech. She was wiping her brow with a square of cambric as she emerged.

"Your friend is quite strange," she announced. "I have never been one of those mothers who puts her foot down about a daughter's choice of close friends, but I ought perhaps to have considered doing so in this case. Should Torin marry her, he might occasionally agree with that judgment. Indeed his life with her would be fraught with interest."

"Was she rude?"

"One does not have to be rude if one is disjointed in speech, my dear Cressy. Your friend seems to feel that wagering, which she is convinced we do for pleasure (and how we have been able to hide our tracks from that argus-eyed miss, I will never know. She may have been blinded over the years by friendship and affection) is nothing less than the devil's tool."

"That is an *idée fixe* of hers."

"Coming to the major item on my agenda, she agreed that protracted losses from Dunster's steeds and his tenant farmers would imperil the man's income. He is not among the very wealthy, but has some money in reserve. That amount is what Miss Wyse refers to as barely adequate."

"I am not sure what the phrase means in her terms."

Mama nodded, sadly agreeing with Cressida's estimate of Amaryllis Wyse as a disseminator of truth.

"I hope that your mind is now relieved about Jemmy Dunster's future."

"I am willing to concede only that nothing I do at this juncture will halt the course of events," said Mama, sparing her energies for any effective possible use in the next days. "Let the dance continue."

CHAPTER TWENTY

Supper was served at a slower pace at Lord Dunster's home in Shropshire. Mutton soup had probably turned lukewarm while being apportioned out to the diners on Tuesday night. The boiled capons could probably have moved more quickly to each place under their own steam, dead though they were. Warm carrots and peas were served alongside the capon. This was followed by a Charlotte russe of fruit crusts and meringue topping. To have served lukewarm tea would have been inexcusable even in the sight of a master without a wife, so the tea was scalding hot.

The only female who was usually to be found at table was perhaps nine years old and named Francesca but known as Tootles. His lordship's sister was a merry-eyed child at that stage of life in which she continually asked questions and had to be quelled by strong words. None of her questions, on this summery night, at least, had anything to do with the meal.

Dunster, sitting at the head of the table under one of the bright red Chinese lanterns that served for illumination, spoke when he had to. Even while addressing one of the others, his eyes remained fixed on Cressida.

She had come to the table feeling confident of her attractiveness. Her crinkled silk with its pin-dotted brocading was effective, along with her touched-up features and freshly washed and combed blond hair. She was prepared to exchange glances continually, and even answer him in words with two meanings. Success at such an endeavor would have been unusual for her. Instead she found herself confronting the knowledge that his eyes hardly left her. No female ever looked attractive while eating. To test her in this would have been bruising to the amour-propre of Madame Pompadour.

His lordship turned away after Torin said something in a constricted voice. The words concerned a racing paper that he hoped to start. Papa responded cuttingly. Mama spoke with her usual deference, but in such a way that the quarrel was not going to be pursued at this table.

His lordship looked keenly at the older man and then said, "I believe you knew my late guv'nor, sir."

"Indeed I did," Papa said with warm agreement. "A man who took land for himself the way some children take the toys of others. He was a credit to his peerage, his Queen, and his nation."

"I believe that you knew my mother before she married. She was a Miss Cattermole."

"I did indeed know Elizabeth Cattermole, your lordship. A lovely woman with the most beautiful light gray eyes."

Dunster, who had apparently inherited these, closed his own eyes for a moment.

"Dancing with her was a great pleasure, as she was lighter than a feather."

"My mother spoke of you often, and sometimes with regrets that you had never asked for her hand."

"Ah." Papa smiled to himself.

Mama, listening with astonishment, gazed at her husband with a certain new respect. The fresh attitude was not lost upon the Fleet children.

"I have sometimes wondered," said Dunster, easing his forefingers into vest pockets of the dark brown twill Melton suit, "if there was anything more to your acquaintance than an occasional dance."

"Sir, there was not," Papa said flatly. "And if there had been, I would not be prepared to say so."

Dunster nodded, far from surprised by such an attitude. There was a moment's silence caused by respect for the social ethics of Hartley Fleet. The Fleet siblings appeared stunned by the knowledge that their father could so much as make a decision for himself, let alone one that was important as well as admirable.

Mama murmured several words in such a tone that she must have been cynical. Presumably she spoke to herself against Papa, which she had rarely done aloud in the presence of the children or of company.

Papa drew himself up, still aware of having been admired. Spurred by that reflection, he spoke his mind.

"You may be thinking that you have been cheated by fate, my dear, but you have received a great domestic gift from me."

Mama looked carefully at him.

"It is the gift of an excuse," Papa responded. "Should you be rude to one of the children or step on a stranger's feet, should you be thoughtless or your behavior ill-considered, the Sociables know the reason. You are permitted to show fierce resentment of others because of the domestic situation in which you find yourself and the lack of your husband's wealth. In that sense, my dear, you are a free woman and only because of the gift you have had from me."

He met her eyes with a directness that would have done credit to their daughter. It was Gladys Fleet who turned away.

Cressida had been waiting for many years to be a witness when Papa showed anger at his wife. Never before had he done so, and such forebearance had seemed disturbing, even unnatural.

Small wonder she spared a smile for Torin and gave a great grin to the impassive Dunster.

Cressida chose to wear a riding outfit the next morning, although she knew perfectly well that she wasn't going to see any horse from the top down. Dunster had made it clear last night that almost no riding for pleasure's sake was done on the estate. Just before the family went up to bed early because the day's excursion had been tiring, he had invited her to see the morning tryouts after her breakfast.

She had agreed before the last word was out of his mouth.

It needed two maids to put her boots where they belonged early on Wednesday. A third helped her into the balance of this rig. The delays were caused by her impatience. Descending in a hurry, she found some difficulty gliding away from dogs and cats of various breeds. Luck alone brought her to the breakfast room at ten minutes past nine without damage to limbs.

Torin and Tootles were helping themselves from the sideboard. The latter was persuaded to stop hurling questions long enough to answer one.

"Jemmy is finished with his food and out at the stables," she said in one breath; and then, "Why do you want to know?"

Cressida shrugged it away. His lordship had already been wakened, had his window curtains pulled aside, his bath filled, and brushed clothing set out. With breakfast and a perusal of his mail having both been concluded, he was now most likely discussing the day's work with stable hands or the head lad.

Cressida yearned to be with him, but she had first to give in to the demands of hunger. She put down sausages and muffins and tea despite a drumfire of questions from Tootles.

Torin, she observed, wasn't looking excessively contented. Most likely he'd considered asking for a loan to start the racing paper he planned. Persistent elders had finally convinced him of one truth: Dunster's finances weren't such that he could afford to lend considerable money and continue eating three good meals a day.

The lure of the stables, as long as Jemmy was near them, beckoned even more strongly. She rushed out of the main house with its gray stone covered by creeping roses, and looked around anxiously.

Everything in sight was certainly well-kept. To her right was the center park with perfectly tended oaks and beeches and Lombardy poplars, as well as smooth-shaven grass upon which antlered deer grazed decorously. Beyond this, on a slight decline, she could see the tidy straw roof of the gatekeeper's lodge. In the distance was a hayrick, probably belonging to that tenant whose home was closest. Past that, from the village of Little Pilkington, shone the steeple of the Norman parish church. Clouds had respectfully avoided defacing the sky. It was a dewy morning after the slightest touch of rain, and almost everything in sight appeared to have been tinted so as to deepen the natural colors.

A beautiful morning without a flaw.

"Where are you going?" asked Tootles.

The child had apparently been following. Every feature of her face was slightly altered by curiosity.

"I thought I would walk about," Cressida answered with an appearance of serenity.

The little monster chuckled. "Jemmy is at the stables."

Because the child was intruding and not a fully formed adult, her movements reminded Cressida of the ever-awkward Charley's Aunt in the play of that name. This was a very young Dona Lucia D'Alvadorez.

"Perhaps I shall see your brother."

"Can I join you?"

There was no way to prevent the child from stalking her, like a red Indian in one of the books that Torin had read as a boy.

"Only if you'll promise not to ask any questions along the way."

"Very well. Do you think I ask too many—"

"Tootles!"

"All right, I'll put a sock in it." The child must have been told more than once that she'd better find other ways to irritate adults.

Tootles led the way down a road that took them past the kitchen garden. Domestic vegetables of every known sort were in the ground, their beds bordered by box and privet hedges. The trees that served for wall-fruit held apple and apricot and peach and plum and pear, as well as cherry. Greenhouses, grape houses, peach houses, and forcing frames had been set down at the farthest end. Bees in their hives, like everything else in Dunster's demesne except for Tootles, were beautifully behaved.

Cressida was growing impatient by the time they passed the trio of tennis courts, hardly caring that these were as smooth and level and green as those tables at which gentlemen played billiards. Instead of finding herself closer to Jemmy Dunster, she felt as if she was making her way through some bizarre forest, which held every modern convenience.

She heard the hoofbeats of horses on a track and looked to her right. The track wasn't in view, but she could at least see the stables. These formed a quad, with a paved court in the center. Her guide encouraged Cressida to enter through an archway and below a clock that suddenly chimed as if to mark the occasion.

On the other side of the stables, a two-turn racing course had been constructed.

"You did indeed find the way," said Jemmy Dunster by way of greeting.

He was smiling warmly as he emerged from a paddock. He

wore boots larger than hers, to be sure. He wore knife-creased trousers and a straw hat, with an unadorned white shirt between them. Clearly he was blessed with health and strength. If Tootles hadn't been among those present, Cressida told herself, she might simply have melted into his sturdy arms.

The child snickered at something that, incredibly, she must have found amusing.

Jemmy's attention was directed to her. "Where are your boots, creature?" he demanded. "Return instanter for them."

"Can't I—I mean, may I—I mean, I would like to be permitted to stay."

"You can join Miss Fleet and myself just as soon as you are properly dressed."

Cressida's eyes followed his, inspecting the track and assessing the results of the recent contest. A pair of horses had been racing. Lady Fortune, who could be recognized by the blinders, had calmly accepted defeat. The finer-looking beast, rather than glorying in victory, was now snorting in attempts to break the grip of the handler of its reins.

Dunster started to the track, where he was joined by his head lad. This was a man with gray hair and chin whiskers. Not only was he far from a lad, as such, but his appearance gave the lie to the conviction that an outdoors vocation makes a man slim. He seemed to have devoted his life to crushing the illusions of others.

"You can't really judge performance by a dirt track," he was saying, "not even this one."

"The dirt is firm and as good as grass," Dunster responded, a point that Cressida confirmed by stepping gingerly upon it with one boot.

"For the energy he's using, I wish he was eating better," the head lad said dourly.

"He's eating well, and that's the point."

"But look how hard to handle he is."

"It's a sign that he might be approaching the peak of condition," Dunster pointed out, and surprisingly looked to Cressida for confirmation. "High-spirited, as you can see."

It was the handler who agreed, but not with satisfaction. "He feels like he wants to kill. I'm sorry for whoever's going to ride him this Saturday."

Cressida couldn't help interrupting. "Wasn't anybody riding him just now? I ought to have noticed, but somehow I didn't."

"No one was riding either horse, Miss." The head lad spoke while the handler shook his head. Both men were among the most pessimistic of Irish folk that Cressida had ever encountered.

She turned accusingly to Dunster.

"Miss Cressida," said the peer, irritated. "As a dilettante who is a patron of the races, you cannot expect to understand the finer points of training."

"Please clarify the procedure for me, using only the simplest words. Why do you train a horse by letting him—or her, I presume—ride without the weight that has to be carried during a race?"

"Because it allows freedom for a horse to be ponied instead of galloped. The horse comes to learn what is possible and is not aware of burdens, which have to be accepted as an added irritation when that becomes necessary."

"Or the animal comes to feel that the full weight is an unfair and intolerable burden."

"Society Scandal [as this animal has been named] is not always ponied, you may be sure."

"But I gather it happens far too often. The animal doesn't know until he's about to be raced that he must carry such accessories as a bridle and saddle, a surcingle, a stirrup iron, a shadow roll, and—oh yes—a rider. You want him to accept the possibility that he doesn't have to race without carrying the necessary burden of his full weight, and that is a falsehood."

"In your view, a horse should know nothing of pleasure," Dunster said briskly. "Its whole life should be an example of (What is that poetry? Ah yes) 'Duty, stern daughter of the voice of God.' Permit me to inform you that an animal is in need of happiness, just as many humans are."

The quarrel, if allowed to proceed, would be unpleasant as well as long. It would take time, as she appreciated, from the necessary training.

"Thank you for permitting me to inspect some of your horses

and learn for myself how they are handled," Cressida said evenly, unable to avoid the slightest of accents on that last word.

"You will appreciate Society Scandal far better when he wins at Hexham on Saturday," said Dunster in conclusion.

"For your sake, your lordship, I hope he does win," Cressida said sincerely. "I am also coming to feel that a part of your overall judgment is correct: in racing matters, one of us is a dilettante."

CHAPTER TWENTY-ONE

The living room of the Dunster manse was reached through an anteroom by way of the Great Hall. On Thursday night it was crowded with local friends who had come to attend a gathering.

It did seem to Cressida's startled ears that the Shropshire side of the River Severn was populated not so much by the Welsh as by Scottish peers and their wives. Most of the men cast admiring looks at her.

Rarely had she appeared so attractive. She was dressed in pleated rose-and-black silk, each fold kept in place by a gleaming button. Where white cravats were locally fashionable, she had determined to show decolletage instead.

Mama had said encouragingly, "It will perk up your spirits as well as the men's eyes, Cressy."

It seemed not to have affected Dunster, who was talking to friends as if he didn't know that any Fleets were in the room. He had been no more than courteous to her since yesterday morning's overheated discussion. Cressida would have approached him without hesitation, but he was in the company of his young sister. Tootles could be depended on to say something that strangers had no business knowing.

"Francesca is a sensible young woman," Dunster was telling another guest as he looked down proudly at the child. "She will grow out of her current juvenile fancies and become a fine wife to some exceedingly wealthy young man—or so I hope."

"I am sure it will happen in just that way," said a fashionably dressed female—who hadn't yet looked away from Dunster—in impeccably cut evening wear.

"After all, a grown woman doesn't spend her time in rereading *Under Two Flags* and imagining herself as Cigarette, as I think it is, who steps before a firing squad and saves the life of Lord Bertie Cecil."

Tootles started, "But don't you remember—?"

There was a stir as the butler entered with half a dozen footmen, each carrying a golden tray holding liquid refreshments. Any dereliction of an underling would certainly be noted by Crouch, the butler, in spite of his foggy square-shaped glasses.

Cressida had been trying to show polite interest in the conversation of a peer. He could talk about nothing but the recent sales of Hereford sheep down at Craven Arms. Cressida found that her capacity to be absorbed by this subject was rather slight.

Dunster had left that woman and was now introducing Mama and Papa to various owners of racing horses. Cressida was turning to join them when Torin halted in front of her.

"I am sorry to hear about your dispute with our host as far as Society Scandal is concerned." His intelligent bright blue eyes were fixed on her. "Do you truly feel that he cannot win at Hexham on Saturday?"

Distracted, Cressida paused to answer him. "I have seen too many horses win unexpectedly, so I cannot be definite. But in the case of Society Scandal, a victory seems unlikely."

"I am inclined to say that victory is as likely as defeat, Cressy. This afternoon I watched him run with a rider on him and all the fixin's, as the Yankees say."

For once she didn't tell him as an aside that it was occasionally unnerving to hear him speak American slang with a London accent.

"Even after having seen that steed with the proper impedimenta," she pointed out, "you remain uncertain about his chances at Hexham."

"Whether he performs well or not, Cressy, depends on the quality of the other horses who are mixing in, as they say in

Yankeeland. What I'm suggesting is that he could make it. It's possible."

"Your objection is noted, as they doubtless say in the local law court of quarter-sessions." Cressida kept from asking about the state of his relations with Amaryllis Wyse. The consultation, as Kenneth Baldro would have called it, might have gone on till morning. "Please, excuse me."

Papa and Mama were fully occupied in talk with a man whose Scottish accent was as clear as the general subject of conversation was inevitable. "The public may deserve to see the best horses, but no one will ever convince me that a gelding merits participation in any important race."

At her right, on the way to greet some other guest, was Dunster. Tootles hurried at his side. There was no third party to overhear any remark that the child might make. Cressida's heart was pounding as she started to move in front of Dunster with the intention of cutting him off from others in the room.

Tootles saw her first. Inevitably, she asked a question. "Don't you think I should be allowed to stay after the music has improved me spiritually?"

Cressida couldn't help smiling. "I think that you look very well (which would certainly be the answer to your next question), but that by now you should already be in bed."

Dunster had turned. It was impossible to identify the play of feeling on those handsome features. Almost as if he had seen an unwelcome presence, but a decidedly attractive one.

Cressida, to be sure, spoke first. "I hope that you weren't angered by yesterday morning's discussion between us."

"Not angered, no," Dunster said slowly as he considered the matter. "I was astonished."

"Don't you recognize the possibility that people with knowledge may differ?"

"Certainly, but you sounded as if your opinion was as valid as mine. I must point out yet again that you and your family are merely interested in the racing course as an amusement. I, on the other hand, am fully occupied by its procedures and foibles. I mean no disrespect, but that distinction gives my opinion a certain value to which yours cannot aspire."

Once more she wished to herself that it was possible to enlighten him about her family's need for success at the course. She always wanted to tell the truth, whether to a stranger or a possible husband. Although such a response was out of the question at this time, she spoke her feelings about the crucial phase of the difference between them.

"You are apparently saying that we have opposed each other too often for you to ever be contented in my presence."

Dunster shouldn't have been taken aback. Nevertheless, he drew away. Only then did he narrow his eyes in thought. It had been brought home to him that his attitude was wholly unreasonable.

"For whatever it may be worth to you, your lordship, I say yet again that I hope Society Scandal wins. I truly hope that he does."

Before Dunster could thank her or respond in any way, a silence began to spread in the room. Clearly the musical portion of the evening was about to be unleashed. Dunster had no choice but to proceed with Tootles to the front row of chairs that had been set in place during the last moments. His figure, as seen from the back, was that of a self-assured man with a healthy body.

Herr Waldemar Stoeckel, the celebrated concert pianist, entered from the anteroom. The small but burly artist walked in portentous silence to the Bechstein at the northeast end of the room. He struck the keys as if he hated them, but several musical chords were produced in a pleasing sequence.

Cressida had found a place for herself. She sat next to Torin on one side and Mama on the other. Dunster was out of her view. The music filling her ears was that of *Till Eulenspiegel's Merry Pranks*. She tautened her lips, not being in the mood for pranks.

Tips to the servants were given out after breakfast on Friday morning. Papa passed a full sovereign to Crouch and three shillings to each of the footmen who had waited upon him or Torin in their rooms. Mama, for her part, disbursed three shillings to each of the ladies' maids who'd assisted her and Cressida. The total for their added expenditures was small, as the Fleets hadn't used such facilities of the grounds as were available to those who visited during the autumn. There had been no call upon the services of the gamekeeper, nor was any game being sent on to them in London.

Dunster made no appearance to say farewells. Cressida assumed that such neglect of guests must be his final answer to the amende honorable she had made last night before the onslaught of merry pranks.

Tootles had appeared, however. She wore a striped tennis gown that made her look more like a gnome than a female who was small and youthful. The purchase of such a rig-out for a child could only have been approved by a male.

She managed to speak four sentences without ending one of them in a query.

"Jemmy says that I must apologize to you all because he isn't here. He's at the stables. Tomorrow he has to race Society Scandal. He wants to attend to any matters that might come up at the last minutes of preparation." And then she backslid: "Do you understand what I mean?"

She was looking particularly at Cressida, for whom the message was apparently most importantly intended.

Papa said grandly, "Please convey our best wishes to your brother. Tell him that we are deeply in his debt for our having learned so much about racing matters."

With her head high, and not looking from left to right, Cressida led the way out of the house and down a slight incline toward the gatekeeper's lodge. The Fleet family carriage, with Daymore up, was waiting to take them home. It was a superb spring day. Mama, who loved birds, spent part of the walk identifying a mussel thrush, a ring ouzel, and a chiffchaff. Just before they reached the gate she called out with pleasure at the unexpected sight of a pied wagtail.

CHAPTER TWENTY-TWO

"You cannot pass the balance of your life in punishing pillows," Mama remarked.

The point was well taken. Upon returning home to Albemarle Street, Cressida had ascended to her room and occupied herself by striking each of the pillows with a fist. The place probably looked like Tootles's idea of the scene of a massacre as it might have been described in *Under Two Flags*.

"I know I have to prepare my charts for tomorrow's races," Cressida said moodily. "I would just as rather that the meeting took place in hell than in Hexham."

"To the people who lived there during the time of Hadrian's Roman wall, I doubt if there was much difference. However, it is not racing that I have come here to discuss. Nor will I do more than express my regrets over what may be a setback to your future plans, Jeremy Dunster's recent responses (as you tell me) having been so wrong-headed."

It did seem as if Mama was genuinely regretful. Cressida nodded in appreciation, then quirked her brows in curiosity which must shortly be satisfied.

"I have arranged, with your papa's approval, to compensate us briefly on this night for all the recent irritations. We are to enjoy a singular treat. There have been showings, as they are called, of motion pictures in New York City since last year. Tonight, there will be one in London, and we are to attend."

Cressida was willing to oblige her elders by putting in an appearance at that rite.

"Must I dress?"

"I see nothing incorrect in looking your best for any occasion, no matter how strange."

The performance was to take place at a theater redundantly called the Royal Empire. It was located on Church Street in sight of St. Mary Abbott's, the parish church of Kensington. Although the location and surroundings were far from fashionable, the theater seemed to be filled from top to bottom with Sociables.

"This was performed in New York for the first time shortly before I arrived," Torin said so proudly that Cressida inferred he had been the prime mover in an effort to have the family view this forthcoming spectacle. "I didn't have the opportunity to see Mr. Addison's new invention out there, unfortunately."

"*Whose* new invention?"

"A Yank named Thomas Addison, from a county called New Jersey." Torin spoke firmly. On matters of American culture he would accept no correction.

Cressida looked around in vain hopes of discovering Jeremy Dunster. At the same time, Torin was hunting for the sight of Amaryllis Wyse.

It was Torin's search that was rewarded. He excused himself, and was smiling reminiscently when he strode back to join the family. He took that seat at the end of the aisle.

A man stepped onto the stage of the darkened theater and began to talk loudly. Cressida heard very few of his words because Torin was also speaking, in his case about the sweet nature always shown by Miss Wyse. He resented being signaled into silence, not liking to give way to the demands of a stranger.

"One of the marvels of our age," shouted the man in the soup-and-fish, describing this night's entertainment. The wine-red curtains parted as he turned. Cressida rather missed the sight of those curtains, as she could imagine using the color and pattern for a winter day dress.

Her mind was soon diverted by the appearance of the stage. Two colored lights played across what looked like a huge bed-sheet suspended in air. Those lights quickly disappeared, leading to a moment's total silence.

This was broken by someone in the audience who called out, "And now we shall see an elephant performing a dance."

Cressida thought she recognized the high voice of the Honorable Osgood Nisbet, that M.P. who was a friend of Dunster's.

There was no reason to think that Jemmy might show up here as well, but she couldn't keep the notion from her head. Instinctively she looked around, but darkness made it impossible to see who was nearby.

The dark was pierced by a cone of light from a window in a booth far above. A series of gasps sounded from different members of the audience, causing Cressida to turn back and find out what was so startling.

She saw it quickly enough. An image of two girls had appeared on the bedsheet, or whatever might be the name of that contrivance above the stage. Both females were light-haired, but their dresses were patterned differently. As Cressida started in common with everyone else, the figures moved forward and then back. Each motion was clearly defined. The images were apparently performing in rhythm, and it soon became apparent that they were engaged in the celebrated umbrella dance.

"Amazing!" breathed a woman nearby.

There was more to come, but only after the bedsheet had again been darkened briefly. The image of a man appeared, his lips moving and hands outstretched in such a way as to make it plain that he must have been singing.

This was followed by three performers with acrobatic motions. One of them dangled from a trapeze that moved dizzyingly. There was an unplanned diversion as the bedsheet image grew fuzzy. The performance was halted.

The man in the soup-and-fish emerged once more to inform the audience solemnly that the performance would resume shortly.

In the pause, Cressida turned to communicate her wonder and found that Torin was not in his seat. No doubt he had left for some impromptu tête-à-tête with his light o' love, Amaryllis.

On her other side, Mama was discussing the apparitions with Papa. "All of the persons we saw are hidden behind the sheet and perform on cue. It is an illusion, no more."

"The figures are of a greater height than any person we will ever see."

"Mirrors must have been placed to give such an appearance in the eyes of those who are credulous," Mama responded, ever sensible. "What we see there, Mr. Fleet, is impossible on its own terms."

"Time will vindicate one of us," Papa said with the calmness he had adopted since the family's return from Shropshire. He leaned over toward his daughter. "You will live to see many, many marvels, Cressida."

"And let us hope," Mama put in with a sniff, "that some of them will be useful."

She heard a stir in the next seat and turned. Critical words froze on her tongue. The man who had seated himself was not Torin. She was looking directly at Lord Jeremy Dunster.

"I arranged with your brother to transpose seat locations as soon as feasible." He was smiling in such a way as to have melted the heart of a statue. Not for the first time Cressida told herself it had been worthwhile refusing a dance with the Prince of Wales to have remained with this peerless peer.

While praising herself she thanked the gods for having seen to it that she followed her maid's insistence that she change her hairstyle. She had never before worn it in deep waves at the sides, and a supporting chignon in the back. She felt reservations at first, but one result had been to give her appearance a welcome freshness.

Dunster took the time to greet Mama and Papa, then turned back toward her and spoke softly. It seemed unlikely that he'd be overheard.

"I divined that you would appear in the company of Sociables watching this invention, this Bio-scope."

"And how can I be of assistance to you in some way, your lordship?"

" 'Assistance'? You wound me to the quick!"

"I hope not, your lordship, but you have made it amply clear that I am not a companion you would seek out."

"I have said nothing of the sort!"

"Might I ask, then, for the matter to be clarified beyond doubt? I feel it is not too much to hope for."

He drew a deep breath. "Cressida, your view of racing is one and my view is another. I spare you a pitiless analysis of the arguments that clearly sustain—well, my mind has not been changed. What I wish to convey is my deep regret about the difficulty that has come between us."

"I regret it, too," she said softly. She wished that she was capable of dissembling, of playing the fool, of behaving as if she found the entire matter hardly worth a mention.

"I was not able to speak those words during the recent past, but I wanted my feelings to be unmistakable."

"That was my wish, too, as I have said. Thank you."

With difficulty she turned away, having made up her mind not to look at him. Anger and regret caused her heart to hammer.

She stared at the presentation, forcing herself to concentrate. Another picture had appeared. This one showed a path with a stream at one side and a double row of trees. Between them ran what seemed like a cowpath, but was proved by further inspection to be part of the line of a railroad.

From the distance something was moving directly forward. The closer it came, the greater its size. Beyond question, as a moment's reflection proved, it was a train. The train was in motion along the exact center of the image.

Someone in the audience moaned and started to rise, aware of being in front of the oncoming metal juggernaut.

Cressida was shrewder. Common sense made it clear that the scene represented a captured image. Mama to the contrary notwithstanding, the phenomenon in front of her had to be a reproduction.

Nonetheless, her response was automatic. She drew out a hand toward Mama for encouragement. Another hand shot out to the right, where her brother had been sitting.

Before she realized her error, that hand was being comfortingly held, firmly held.

Jemmy Dunster whispered fiercely, "Cressida, Cressida, I could not bear never to see you again."

She turned immediately. Dunster's eyes met hers, then he looked down briefly at the masculine figure of the trainer whose ideas remained rooted. The reluctance he clearly felt was not enough, at this time, to keep him from forcing himself to release her hand.

CHAPTER TWENTY-THREE

Papa must have been stirred by the photographed images of that moving train. They probably impelled him to insist that the family use that mode of transportation to reach Hexham. He ignored the silent anguish of the coachman, Daymore, who probably saw himself being made redundant at his career. Daymore was soon instructed to convey the family to the terminus at King's Cross.

They traveled in a dark-blue carriage of the Great Northern railway. As it was one of the Great Northern's composites, only the middle two of four compartments offered first-class accommodations. Papa bristled at the conception of traveling so near to second- and even third-class passengers. Torin's grievance was that they couldn't travel on the speedier trains, such as the Wild Irishman and the Flying Scotchman.

"No matter how great the speed, there would be no sense to taking the Irish night-mail train," Mama pointed out drily, "let alone proceeding to Edinburgh."

For Cressida, the journey ought to have been restful. The train didn't move at its maximum possible rate of fifty-three miles to the hour, as she knew that such speed would have severely shaken her. An Anglo-Indian Wallah had shared this compartment only long enough to tell a dull story about a *havildar* at Simla. There was no reason, then, for her not to have been perfectly relaxed.

No reason but one.

Mama, after a silence between the females, said pensively, "I fear you may see something of Jemmy Dunster up at Hexham."

"I shall indeed," Cressida agreed emphatically. The gentlemen had gone out to shake up their limbs, as Papa called it, and this conversation was welcome. "I look forward to the sight."

"Aren't you being vengeful?"

"I don't feel that way about it."

"Find another description for your feelings, Cressy, if you can."

"I want to be nearby when he finds out that he will have problems with Society Scandal, just as he has already discovered to be the case with Lady Fortune."

"Yet you will not really enjoy seeing him made aware that he has been in the wrong."

"That is so."

"And I do not see the experience changing the way he feels about you."

"There, too, Mama, I must agree."

"Plainly you are convinced that the prospect of being near him in a difficult mood is far from captivating."

"Yes, Mama."

"Nor will being away from him make you as happy as a child in springtime."

"True, Mama."

"It seems insoluble," Mama said. "I have never known a court-ship to proceed along these lines. Your Aunt Agatha, now dead, alas, warned everyone that when Felix offered for her, she was to be hounded out of accepting the arrangement. The day after she agreed to the marriage after all, she embarked upon one of Mr. Cook's faraway tours. To Egypt, I do believe. Upon returning, she was again unable to resist the man's blandishments and gave herself to him—in marriage, I hasten to add. Mind you, they were extremely happy and they had twelve children, to whom she gave birth and hardly saw again until each was twenty-five years of age, all in the best tradition of the Empire. But that is by-the-by, Cressy. What I started to point out is that the current situation between you and Jeremy is hardly such stuff as dreams are made on."

"I am aware of that, too, Mama."

"Considering that you are so straightforward by nature, it would hardly be a surprise if *you* offered for *him.*"

After a talk that repeated this implied criticism, Cressida had as much as she could do to keep from bursting into tears. By the time Papa and Torin returned, she was back in control of herself.

Cressida became inwardly calm as soon as the racing course was reached. She felt as much at home in one of these places as in her own bedroom on Albemarle Street.

She ventured into the silver ring area along with the family. For the second race, she put down five pounds on Overlook at odds of four-to-one. The horse was not favored to win that contest in which Society Scandal was among the participants. Cressida carried the ticket in a hand, expecting the chance to show Jemmy that she had sagely placed her bet upon the eventual winner.

No one she knew was nearby when she left the ring. Mama must have been several feet behind, as often happened at the race course. Torin and Papa had gone off somewhere, perhaps separately. She would have liked to be in someone's company if only for a few minutes.

Her wish was granted, but it wasn't Jemmy who appeared as she walked toward the railing. It was the spirit of bad cheer himself, Mr. Kenneth Baldro, who materialized before her.

"You have purchased a ticket for the very first race," the alienist said in that customarily lugubrious manner, which must have caused many a client to want to defenestrate herself from his chambers.

She discovered that she wanted to cheer him, if only slightly.

"Not for the first race."

She didn't explain that the odds were dismal. A bet of a guinea would have earned no more than sixpence. The family didn't venture enough at each outing to make such a speculation worthwhile.

"You must follow the advice you have been given," the alienist lectured sternly. "This time, you will wager on no more than six races. Next time on only five, and the time after that—well, you recall the entire program I laid out for you after consulting with some of the finest brains in Vienna."

Cressida wasn't paying attention to him, looking around at others in hope of discovering a sight of Dunster. The alienist, for his part, was preening himself in the event he was observed and recognized by a passing Sociable. It would have been difficult for two people to be less aware of each other.

She didn't think of him again until she was turning away.

"We must endure a hiatus now," the alienist said, his voice raised.

Mr. Baldro looked pensively after the young woman in her checked tan gown with the yellow straw hat on her head. Most attractive. It would have been a matter of interest, too, if he had found out something about the young lady's past. Particularly he'd have liked to know in detail just what foods she had been given as an infant. There, as he saw it and had said to her a while ago, lay the roots of her obsession. It would, of course, be a great help to trace its formation.

Briefly he imagined the reaction to his completed paper. His praises would be sung with Viennese accents by every colleague in the valhalla of his discipline. The Baldro theory. Perhaps the Kenneth Baldro theory. Future patients would be diagnosed in relation to the effect on their lives of Kenneth Baldro's theory.

Up to this moment, in the case before him, he had done as much as possible.

He turned away, planning to rejoin Miss Amaryllis Wyse, who had been kind enough to accompany him on this expedition.

Miss Wyse was involved in a discussion with some young man. Her mother, Lady Beryl, who had escorted them, was free. Mr. Baldro advanced toward the older woman, not forgetting to look encouragingly to his right and left as he moved.

Cressida had borrowed Mama's pearl-gray opera glasses. She didn't usually care to depend on an artificial aid to keen sight, but this occasion was special. She had determined to follow the battle between Society Scandal and Overlook.

She rather liked Overlook as soon as he appeared for the march to the barrier. He was one of those aggressive animals with a damn-your-eyes spirit, a fighter from the first paces. Every move reflected a determination to win. The jockey was a beetle-browed young man who looked as if he had recently committed murder and was seeking someone else to accuse of the deed. A well-matched pair, Overlook and his rider.

Society Scandal, approaching the barrier, seemed not so much aggressive as disturbingly irritable. He might have been performing a dance. After every forward step, his body jiggled. Possibly, as Cressida had suggested, he felt he was under too many restraints. The august-looking two-year-old resembled a general on the parade ground in spite of some minor indisposition. The sight wasn't calculated to gladden the heart of any knowledgeable bettor who had made an investment on him.

The other contestants hardly seemed worth noticing. Most of them carried excessive amounts of weight. Cressida didn't trust animals who had been overfed, and she was almost as wary of lean ones. There were weights that didn't seem awkward for some given animals. The oily-coated Overlook was a fine example. So was Society Scandal, proving that Jemmy did use some sense in handling the animals he raced.

The race began, followed by a collective shout from hundreds of throats. Cressida raised her opera glasses immediately, concentrating only on numbers two and three. Overlook, number two, was already leaving the other animals behind in an early lead. Society Scandal was bringing up a lackadaisical third.

Contention, the favorite, rode between them and no more than three lengths back of Overlook, on whom he was closing in. But he seemed to move too heavily on one slightly arthritic foot. His rider became frantic and used the whip accordingly. It was no surprise to see Contention drop behind.

On two sides of Cressida, less than a dozen watchers cursed. Several started to shred their betting vouchers without further delay. That was a mistake. It was almost impossible to know at this stage of a race just what a horse might accomplish in the last tense minutes.

And then Society Scandal made his move. He was showing why his forty outings on different courses had resulted in twenty-six wins or second-places. Cressida had sensed a certain belligerent quality in the animal, but without suspecting that today's event would show it in action.

For Society Scandal, as it turned out, was a stretch runner. Until the turn, presumably, he would use his time to smell the air or recall some proverb that was supposed to help build character. Refreshed and ennobled, he would then move up furiously on the horse that was coming first.

Overlook's rider, having heard the viewers creating a fresh roar, rose further in his saddle and glowered back at Society Scandal.

The two animals were not neck-and-neck in the moments that followed, but Society Scandal's head was certainly parallel with the pommel of Overlook's saddle. Overlook was moving very slightly to the left in hopes of cutting off Society Scandal's opportunity. Both riders' whips were raised, but neither was in use. Nothing that the riders were doing, as far as Cressida could see, had any taint of the illicit.

By this time she was holding the opera glasses so tightly that she thought one of the pearls had moved and a finger was pressing directly against part of the metallic frame. She didn't think she was breathing, a medical marvel that would have strongly impressed Kenneth Baldro.

Overlook came in first, followed by a surly-looking Society Scandal.

Cressida could not have told with any truth how the outcome had affected her feelings. True, she had once again been proved right and that in itself was gratifying. But her capacity to discern winners would not be so impressive to Jemmy Dunster. It might give active rise on his part to considerable resentment.

On all sides, men and women were moving to the silver ring to put down wagers for race number three. Cressida had made up her mind to watch the horses on their way to the barrier for this one, and then instruct her family whether or not to bet, and on which animal.

Instead of coming forward to join her, both parents were deep in conversation with another.

She halted in mid-step, a move that reminded her of the arthritic motion made by Contention in the recent encounter. The third figure could be recognized from his trim back alone. He had come up from the clubhouse to greet these recent guests at his home.

She was undecided whether or not to come closer. A move to her right would at least let her see that splendid profile and more of this familiar fine figure of a man.

Mama, seeing that movement from the corner of an eye, gestured for Cressida to come forward.

"Cressy is here," she said, not one to deny the obvious.

Jeremy Dunster turned. His eyes glinted warmly at sight of her, but his voice was as calm as if he had just seen a mere acquaintance.

"Ah, Miss Cressida, you were right about the identity of one loser in the second race."

Mama said proudly, "Cressy, indeed, put down a wager on the winning horse. There is no use hiding such a light under a bushel. Cressy, show Lord Dunster your voucher and let him see for himself that you're so very clever."

Mama must have known that Cressida wouldn't gainsay the truth of this matter.

She admitted to having won, but only by a nod rather than proudly showing the voucher. "I didn't anticipate that when your horse was aroused he would show such a capacity to run."

"Not to run quickly enough, I fear."

His politeness matched hers. They had apparently embarked on a competition to find out who would be more modest, more self-effacing. What she actually wanted was to feel his lips against her hair, his cheek on hers. The images that came unbidden were most disconcerting, as she wasn't usually a prey to such fantasies.

As if from a distance, she was aware of Papa's voice.

"Something has happened," he was saying with concern in his tones. "I shall garner details from one or more of the bookmakers."

Cressida was aware that the new development must concern the outcome of a preceding race. Nevertheless, she couldn't keep from inspecting his lordship's tanned features one by one and then together. Nor, in all this time, had Jemmy's light gray eyes moved as much as a millimeter from the sight of her. The prevailing feelings between them, clearly, showed a certain amity.

Nothing would have altered, even if she told him the information that her family insisted on not repeating. He couldn't help but feel that such knowledge as hers, gained by application and hard work, must be that of an outsider as it hadn't involved any direct dealing with the animals or travail in handling them. In its dimensions the difficulty seemed worthy of the pen of a Shakespeare.

Papa's face had fallen as he came back. From good manners learned and remembered, he mustered a smile.

"The news is excellent for you, your lordship. Not, I fear, for the family."

Jemmy did turn now, but there was a perceptible pause. Once again he was the alert trainer and owner, this time seeking news from the front.

Which Papa supplied, without further ado. "Overlook has been disqualified on the ground of excessive crowding."

Cressida said simply, "It is Society Scandal's race, then, your lordship. I do indeed congratulate you."

"Thank you, Miss Cressida. I fear it cannot be considered an unalloyed victory."

"Anyone who has wagered upon him is the winner, as are your coffers," Mama pointed out immediately. "Why shouldn't the horse be the winner himself?"

"Because Overlook was in front of him at the race's end, ma'am." Dunster turned. "Your choice was a perspicacious one, Cressida. Indeed I commiserate with you upon the loss, though you and your family can certainly afford it."

He made his farewells and strode off to descend to the lower level. He would shortly be accepting a winner's cup from the judges. More importantly, two other horses of his would be running this afternoon. Sociabilities could take up only a small amount of his time.

Cressida looked after him and then gestured for her elders to follow her toward the rail. The parade to the barriers would soon be under way for the next race, and she had to be alert if she was going to confirm her opinion about the best choice to win.

She gained two unquestioned victories of her judgment by the end of the seventh race. Venturing more money on the others seemed bootless. The best horse in race number eight had been injured during the day, and the others wouldn't cross the finish point in less than a month.

Torin hadn't been in her sight since shortly after the family's arrival. Now he fell in behind the others as they moved toward the principal exit. He walked slowly, listlessly. He looked almost as if he had unexpectedly fallen out of one of those speedy trains he admired.

"Your afternoon has not been more miserable than mine," she said, falling behind and speaking softly.

"I would wager against you on that point." He looked thoughtful. "Do you suppose that a sufficient amount of damage would result if I threw myself in front of the horses on the track?"

"Not during this next race," Cressida said firmly. "What has befallen you?"

"Amaryllis spoke to me in terms that were frank and open, as politicians say."

"In other words, there has been a quarrel."

"I prefer to think of it as one bitter outburst after another from her. Cressy, you look as if you were about to tell me that the path of true love never runs smooth. I advise you to cease and desist before starting to do so. I am not (let me repeat that in case of misunderstandings) *not*, in a humor for observations of that sort, pithy though they might be."

"Very well. What was the quarrel about?"

"Roughly, about one of the great interests of her life. You know that she has always investigated the financial positions of any family with a member who might be a possible husband for her."

Cressida nearly halted. "You are not going to tell me—"

"Indeed I am. She had never looked into our family's financial position because she didn't consider the possibility of marrying into it. Lately, however, she has spoken to this one and that one. She has put two and two together. The resulting sum, I regret to tell you, is only four."

"Does she know about our collective source of income?"

"It wasn't indicated during her polemic, so I assume that the answer is a resounding no."

"Thank heaven for small mercies."

Torin had failed to ask about her own difficulties. Cressida was already old enough to put down such negligence to a lack of thoughtfulness that was typically masculine.

He was muttering under his breath as the family left Hexham. Cressida remained down in the mouth. The elders, having noted that the day's profits had been small, were irritable. No one spoke unnecessarily. No one looked out of the train window later on. The novelist to the contrary, the members of this unhappy family were all alike.

CHAPTER TWENTY-FOUR

Cressida was sleeping restlessly. Early on Sunday morning, the twenty-first, she turned and reached out a hand for she-knew-not-whom—or wouldn't tell herself whom. The hand touched nothing, as might have been expected. In dismay her eyes flew open.

There was a series of rapid but gentle knocks against the door panel from the hall. The door opened after a pause. Mrs. Durbin, the housekeeper, was looking flurried, bewildered, and apologetic at the same time. It was a combination that might have daunted so fine an actress as Miss Ellen Terry herself.

"You have probably forgotten what day it is," Cressida began generously, always ready to give the benefit of every doubt to the efficient Mrs. Durbin.

"No, Miss Cressida, not at all. It was your mother who suggested that you be asked to join her in the drawing room."

Such a request had been unprecedented since Cressida began predicting the identities of victorious horses. It didn't seem likely that any exception would be made unless there were rabble in the street who thirsted for every Sociable in London to be summarily executed.

"But why does she want my company at this time?"

"Because of the visitor, Miss Cressida."

An image came to her of the sainted Jeremy waiting impatiently. She sat up without delay.

"Send Charity to me immediately," she instructed, referring to one of her maids. "I must dress quickly and superbly."

"No, Miss Cressida, there is no need to dress exceptionally, I can assure you."

She shrugged, hoping that she had hidden the moment's disappointment. Mrs. Durbin knew perfectly well that a young woman dressed superbly on the occasion of a visit by a young man who was unattached and desirable.

"Very well, but send Charity to me all the same. I shall join my mother in the lower drawing room as soon as may be."

She had decided what to wear by the time Charity rushed in. As a result, she reached the drawing room clad in a simple day dress of a shade that some berserk *couturier* had christened burnt rose.

She discovered her mother bemused, and a guest of impeccable calm. The guest was Francesca, known as Tootles, the nine-year-old sister of Lord Jeremy Dunster.

"Are you alone in the city?" Cressida asked promptly.

"Do you think I could reach London by myself? On what train could I get my passage? How would I find this house if I were alone?"

Cressida pursed her lips irritably. Despite tender years, the child seemed to have assimilated the Socratic method of discourse.

It was Mama who put in, "She arrived with a quaking governess who is more like the child's servant than an exemplar of what is right."

"Do you mean Miss Prism?" Tootles was putting up a hand in front of her lips to hide unseemly merriment. "Doesn't she strike you as strong-willed, either? Don't you think she is usually quite correct in deportment? I can assure you of that—but would you like to try speaking with her about handbags? Can you believe that one mention of that word will make her beside herself and quite biddable?"

"Now I have a question for you, young lady: Why have you inflicted yourself upon the London scene this Sunday morning?"

"How could anybody keep from wanting to attend the party?"

Cressida's first instinct was a feeling of sympathy. Like all England, the child wanted to help celebrate the sixtieth year of Queen Victoria's reign. Unlike others from the provinces, Tootles had translated the wish into an action.

"I would now like to find out why you have come to this house."

"Isn't it true that except for Prism, I am alone in London? Don't I therefore have to go to those who will have a place and a better view of the procession than I could possibly obtain? Who else do I know in London who has visited us recently and owes the Dunsters a favor?"

"You will undoubtedly grow up to be one of the very few female pirates in the history of the Spanish Main," Cressida observed. "Does your brother know that you are in this fair community?"

"How could he not know? What else have I done for the last weeks except ask for permission to be taken here and tell him how much I want to see the Queen?"

Cressida had a faint recollection that at some time during the recent visit, when she wasn't sniggering at the prospective pairing of her brother with some female, Tootles had spoken approvingly of the Queen and the forthcoming "party." That had been how she'd referred to the great Diamond Jubilee year procession, which was to take place on this very day.

"Then he hasn't been directly informed," Cressida mused. "That omission must be rectified."

"Do you have to tell him now?" The child's bright eyes were suddenly shadowed.

Cressida hurried to the telephone closet. It took time to make contact with Crouch, the butler at the Dunster holdings in far-off Shropshire. More time drifted past while she waited to hear the master's voice. The interval took long enough for a fit for a new tea gown.

"Cressida? Is that you?"

His voice was at its normal level, which caused her heart to pound more quickly. It was almost as if the two of them were alone in this small area, a thought which made her blush to the very tips of her ears.

"Your sister is here," she said immediately, with the intention of dispelling his worry.

It promptly developed that his lordship had been unaware of the disappearance. He could be heard opening the door of his telephone closet and demanding that Miss Prism be brought to his study without delay.

Cressida said, "The governess accompanied her."

"I shall have words for that lady when she is in my presence once more." The knowledge that his sister wasn't alone in London, however, was enough to soothe his ruffled feathers. "I must say that it sounds almost like a biblical exodus."

"Francesca came to London to see the procession and has asked my family to obtain a grandstand place for her."

"Indeed," said his lordship noncommittally. "I'd have been in the city myself if I wasn't so busy making fresh arrangements for our mutual friend, Lady Fortune."

Cressida vividly remembered the horse riding as poorly with blinders as without. She waited for him to add some acknowledgment of the curious issue that was keeping them from each other's arms. It was in vain.

She resumed the discussion of the matter that was of immediate concern.

"We will send your sister and her governess back by railway after the procession is done, your lordship. They should be arriving by midmorning tomorrow on the Midland."

"Excellent."

There was no reason to speak with him any further. It was difficult to accept the knowledge that she'd no longer hold the receiver tight and feel the tingle of his voice.

"I will now put your sister on the telephone."

"No need," he said unexpectedly. "The facts have been conveyed—and very capably."

"Thank you. All the same she is your sister and has clearly acted against your wishes. You should express the disapproval you feel, but indicate that she won't be subject to reprisals when she comes back."

He made a sound of annoyance, but wasn't committing himself.

"For what I hope is your benefit and hers, your lordship, permit me to say something more," Cressida went on, exactly as if she would have been capable of not speaking her mind. "It would be wise to refrain from calling her 'Tootles' or, as I've heard you do, 'Creature.' She should be addressed as Francesca so as to awaken her to responsibility."

His lordship remained silent.

"I will now put your sister on the telephone."

She returned to the child, who was waiting tensely.

"Come with me, Francesca," she said, "and don't let yourself worry."

"Very well," the child agreed calmly, not making the statement into a question.

The Royal procession to Westminster Abbey was being held on a day that was a perfect example of that phenomenon known to Londoners as the Queen's Weather. Even onlookers with the weakest eyesight and located far off could have made out the horse-drawn open carriage and the small plump woman who was its passenger. Nor could those handicapped onlookers have failed to identify her lace-trimmed black satin, let alone the lace bonnet set with jewels like strawberries on a cake.

Cressida's elders cheered and applauded from their places in the specially built grandstand. Their guest joined in the symbol of affection.

The Fleet siblings, however, stared at nothing. If they felt any strong emotion, it was not apparent.

During a pause in the festivities, Papa took it upon himself to offer some much-needed cheer in that direction.

"Doesn't it make you proud to be British?"

There was a long hesitation, during which a younger Victoria could probably have given birth to a sixth child.

"I suppose so," Torin conceded as if the admission had been forced from him under torture.

"Yes," Cressida said when she was aware of a shift in Papa's inquiring glance. But she was looking away from the procession, which had once more started to move.

"The Queen is a brave woman," Papa said, persevering.

The noise of a moving carriage caused Cressida to look up. She happened to confront the sight of the Queen's three sons and two daughters.

"Yes, she is brave," Cressida agreed.

"That brave woman deserves your plaudits for having sat on the throne of England these sixty years!" Papa sounded like an editorial in some Tory newspaper.

His son was not sympathetic. "The Queen doesn't have to depend upon others before she is able to do whatever she wishes."

Papa, remembering the tenor of his offsprings recent complaints, took another tack.

"The two of you have been bleating about lost love. There, however, is a woman who lost her great love some thirty years ago and has carried on by herself ever since."

Cressida was impelled to look directly at him. "Until then, however, she'd been with the one she loved."

Torin nodded vigorously. "She's had love, and she's done what she liked. She can hardly be considered a model for me. Or Cressy, of course."

Papa drew back with dismay and anger. In another setting he would have made his feelings crystal clear to anyone in earshot.

Mama put a gloved hand on his arm, gently keeping him from the tendency to rumble like a volcano.

Speech was impossible for the next moments. The carriage that was now passing contained the Queen's five in-laws and nine grandchildren.

Mama asked softly, "Cressy, dear, have you noticed the women's superb dresses and cloaks, even the breathtaking bonnets? I say nothing about the Indian cavalry, whose costumes are eye-filling in the extreme. Aren't you at least interested in the clothes on view before you?"

Cressida, as ever, refused to hide her feelings. "No, Mama, I am not at all interested in those things."

"Then it is useless to talk to you," Mama decided immediately.

She spared a glance for her son. Torin's lips were drawn taut. He was making laudable attempts at self-control.

"Mr. Fleet," she said to her husband after the briefest of pauses, "let those who are capable of feeling enjoyment do exactly that. None will be alive forever, but you and I in this family will have happy recollections of a moment in history, which we will be able to call upon throughout eternity."

CHAPTER TWENTY-FIVE

Torin's head was feeling ghastly. It would probably have fallen off his shoulders if he moved too quickly. After which, it was likely to roll around the floor. His eyes were developing a tendency to move about by themselves, sometimes in his head and sometimes not.

He was, in short, a young man recently awakened after a night's carousing.

He had preferred going out to a club last night rather than joining a Jubilee celebration. He happened to know some chap who belonged to the Junior Garrick. Together they went to the Junior Pall Mall, where the friend knew a chap. Three-strong, they marched off to the Junior Whist. All were drinking steadily and pledging undying loyalty to one another until they reached the Junior Conservative near Birdcage Walk.

This friend of a friend was a son of wealth. Most of his talk concerned advice about success in the world of commerce, as if that could be achieved by anyone who was willing to work hard. As if no special entrée was needed. Torin's teeth gritted while he listened.

"Always make sure that others agree with the course of action you have chosen," said Frederick Hollington oracularly. "Discuss the matter in privacy with them before a meeting. Make it clear that what you want is the most sensible course. But be absolutely certain you're right or everything else goes by the boards."

Torin sounded as if he was strangling. It would have been difficult to find advice more useless to a young man with no surfeit of money.

One of the club members appeared at the entrance to the strangers dining room. He was escorting four nonmembers who were guests of his. A smile at Hollington was answered by nothing more than a cool nod.

"An Irish peer," Hollington said disdainfully. "If *they* are admitted to the Junior Conservative, the committee might just as well start letting in Barbary apes." He cocked his head, waiting for agreement.

"I happen to be Irish on both sides of my family," Torin lied, his nerves already stretched to the snapping point. "Faith and begorra, I'm proud of it, me boyo!"

The gauntlet had been laid down. For the only time in its somber history, the Junior Conservative members erupted in a free-for-all. Most of the time these men spoke in the lowest of tones and took only the smallest and most dignified steps when they walked. For a few blessed minutes, adopting one side or the other, they swore like troopers and hurled themselves at the enemy. It was a respite as welcome to them, in its way, as the sixtieth anniversary of the Queen's accession to the throne.

A groggy Torin had returned by growler to Albemarle Street. It was approximately four o'clock in the morning. His clothes were almost shredded and his midriff seemed like one gigantic bruise. His right eye was slightly discolored. Most importantly, though, he had survived the engagement without broken bones. Considering this happy outcome, on balance, he was proud to have fought for the Irish, as he thought of his recent actions.

It was noon when he awakened in his clothes. After changing awkwardly into afternoon wear, he lurched into the guv'nor's bedroom. Here, as he didn't want the sight of him to be a shock to the women of his family, he made a clean breast of last night's occurrences.

The account caused Mr. Hartley Fleet to feel bemused. Foregoing his usual drumfire of criticism in dealing with the boy, he found himself briefly recalling certain long-forgotten episodes of his gilded youth.

"I will inform your mother that you were set upon by marauders and that you fought like a tiger."

"Thank you."

"I suggest that you ask Mrs. Durbin to fix what she calls a bracer." Smiling, the guv'nor added affably, "My wild colonial boy."

Torin managed a descent to the first floor. Too soon he found himself seated alone in the dining room and staring at the liquid concoction that had been brought to him. This, he had no doubt, was the color of his insides. In taste it resembled his idea of gall and wormwood, with just a *soupçon* of wet sand.

It put him in the mood to ask forgiveness for his sins, whatever those might have been.

It put him in the mood to lay on the floor and turn up his toes.

It did not put him in the mood for the presence of his younger sister in some sort of distress. Yet it was this last event to which he was promptly exposed.

"I cannot believe this," Cressida averred, having entered the room and begun pacing back and forth. "I do not believe this."

"I was battling ferociously against the tawdry bigotry of—"

Cressida did not halt her progress to nowhere. "What are you blathering about?"

"I was explaining to you that the wound about my right eye was honorably acquired in a battle for the rights of—"

"This is no time to boast about some fresh depravity of yours, whatever it might have been."

"Cressida, I beg leave to inform you—"

"Stow it!" his sister said abruptly. "Stamp on it and leave it in Piccadilly! Throw it into the Thames!"

Torin realized that his sister didn't want to hear about the example he had set for all humanity. Putting down the last of his bracer, he held on to the table. This allegedly stationary item of furniture was developing an unfortunate tendency to slide out of his reach.

"I am under the impression, Cressy, that something is wrong, in your opinion."

" 'Opinion'? 'Wrong'?"

"Well, it's not with your ears or lips and tongue. You hear well enough to repeat my every fourth word to perfection."

"Bah!"

Torin said mildly, "May I request that you refrain from stomping the length of this room? You sound like a herd of budgies."

Cressida, thinking aloud, didn't desist from pacing. "I tell you that something has got to be done immediately!"

Only then did Torin pose the question he should have raised at the start.

"What has taken place?"

"According to the day's issue of the *Racing Intelligencer*—the special once-a-year walking-ring issue, I may tell you—it is reported that Jemmy has entered his horse, Lady Fortune, at Coniston."

"Oh, and you think that she is sure to lose once again, which will bring yet more grief upon his head. I see at last."

"No, you don't see at all. This special race is to be held on Thursday, three days from now. It's a claiming race."

"What of that? After the day's festivities, horse owners in the audience may bid upon the various animals who just ran. They will buy whichever they desire and can afford. I see nothing wrong with such a *divertissement.*"

"No, you wouldn't. Let me explain so as to make matters unquestionably clear. Jemmy is shopping that horse because he was persuaded against doing any further work with her."

"Whoever did that much, Cressy, would appear to have done him a favor."

"You must remember perfectly well that I am the one who talked against the horse. I said that any future attempts to improve her performance would be useless. Indeed, Jemmy's next try in that direction came to nothing."

"Now that you mention it, I do call to mind your giving me details of the matter."

"Good! I found it hard to believe that you could be so transmuted by love as not to recall the simplest events in the past."

"'Simple'?" Torin was momentarily distracted. "From what you've told me, the matter involved several confrontations."

"If Jemmy keeps Lady Fortune," said Cressida, who wasn't at all distracted, "he will think of me as someone who may have been mistaken, may have given him bad advice."

"Why should you care how he thinks about you? He seems determined not to propose—" In spite of his pain-wracked body, Torin jumped to his feet, abashed. "Cressy, I do beg your pardon."

She nodded, grateful that she wouldn't have to underline the one point that was plain. Her own feelings for Jemmy remained those of someone who loved.

"If he sells the animal, it is possible that he will think badly of me in the future. He may think of me with feelings that are akin to dislike."

"Why? Because he accepted counsel and made a move that was entirely sensible?"

"No, because Lady Fortune's next owner could make her into a prize animal, a true winner."

Torin was bewildered. He sat abruptly, grateful that he was once again anchored.

"Answer me this much, Cressy. Considering what the horse does, how she runs, what could possibly make you think there is any chance that her next owner might turn her into a winner?"

For once in her life, Cressida, absorbed by an overpowering recollection, did not answer directly. "This morning I awoke absolutely parched, you see. While I was drinking water with gratitude, to say the least of it, I realized what has been misunderstood about the animal and how she might accordingly become a sensation of the turf."

Torin saw no reason for his sister's mention of water or thirst in this connection, but ascribed his own confusion to the ravages of his current delicate condition.

"I must make a visit to Shropshire immediately and notify him," Cressida said forcefully. "You must accompany me."

It was beyond Torin's capacities at this time to travel farther than his room. He shook his head without falling off his chair of pain.

"Surely it is easier and quicker to put through a call on the telephone," he ventured.

"I did so earlier this morning. The butler assured me that his lordship would be notified of my call and be returning it shortly. Shortly! Notice that word. I waited in the telephone closet or very near it for as much as an hour. I heard nothing from him, not a word."

"Notify him by the telegraph, then. I am certain that the guv'nor keeps some telegraph forms in the house. You have only to affix sixpennyworth of stamps to the form and write your message, then get it off."

"The telegraph has been known to take a long time. Do you remember the recent newspaper account of a message sent out to *Tinsley's Magazine*, I think it was, which arrived only last week and informed the editor belatedly that the Civil War in America had just been concluded?"

"I hardly think that every telegraph fails to arrive for a period of thirty-two years."

"In this matter, I cannot brook even the chance of delay."

Torin caught himself on the verge of advising her to register a letter and therefore communicate with Dunster via the Royal Mail. The suggestion would have been extremely thoughtless. He didn't want to consider his sister's likely reaction to it.

"Why not put through one more telephone call? Perhaps Jemmy Dunster's butler forgot to give the message over. I see nothing else to be done."

One close look at Torin convinced his sister that a sudden visit to Shropshire at this time was out of the question. She expressed her wishes for his speedy recovery, but only did so while on her way to the door.

Mrs. Durbin entered shortly afterward. Having noted with a satisfied nod that the glass in front of Mr. Torin was now empty, the housekeeper conveyed the message she was bringing.

"There is a visitor for you, sir."

"Tell him that I have just died," Torin said miserably, "and my ashes have been scattered over the racecourse at Goodwood."

"The visitor is a lady. Indeed a lady I am certain you wish to see." Mrs. Durbin smiled. "Miss Amaryllis Wyse is in the lower drawing room and waiting to speak with you."

CHAPTER TWENTY-SIX

Since the time of her early maidenhood, Amaryllis Wyse had been seeking a wealthy husband. She would pursue news of eligible gentlemen and especially of their finances with the tenacity of a bloodhound in the prime of life.

Over the last days, it seemed that her character had altered. At the races in Hexham, as would have been expected, Amaryllis had down-rated Torin Fleet vigorously for being a member of a family with very little money. Such a deception should have caused her to exclude Torin from her thoughts. She ought to have simply forgotten his existence.

It had not happened. She had already seen more of him in the last weeks than of any other young man in her life. After Hexham, she was aware of feeling lonely. There was suddenly no man she could look forward to seeing, no one to populate her dreams.

She had been galvanized by the news that he had taken part in a battle royal at (of all conceivable places) the Junior Conservative Club. Not pausing to telephone, let alone telegraph or send a registered letter as Torin had nearly advised his sister to do in an emergency, she had come running over to be with him.

Torin opened the door swiftly. He left it ajar, as demanded by good form and a concern for the young woman's reputation. His action proved that he was functioning. There would be no necessity to put cold compresses on his face and perhaps cut open his clothes to permit him to breathe easier. In her excitement, she had been confused about measures to be taken in his hour of need.

Torin, for his part, smiled happily at the refreshing sight of this vision in turquoise, her eyes even wider because of concern for him. Deeply stirred, he came forward quickly to draw closer to the angel. He told himself that he felt much better. By force of will alone, he had overcome what must have been only a minor indisposition. It surprised him when he suddenly lost his footing and had to take a chair abruptly.

"I am fine," he said through clenched teeth before the matter of his weakness could be raised by the divinity before him. "I have never felt better in my life."

"But you will—ah, feel even better in time, I trust."

"Your presence is a great help to my spirits. The more I see of you, the better I will feel."

He could hear a young woman's footsteps ascending stairs to reach that area in which the telephone closet was located.

"I can but hope that my sister's spirits will survive these next days," he added heavily.

"Cressida?" Amaryllis had been giving little or no thought to her dear friend's welfare. Having unleashed an alienist upon Cressida, it didn't seem that she could do anything more. "But what else is wrong?"

"Upon calm consideration, I would say that almost everything is wrong."

"I must talk with her."

"If you try it now, she will probably bite your head off at the roots. She almost did that to me, and, like you, I am by no means an ill-wisher."

"You must tell me what has gone wrong."

With such encouragement, Torin embarked on a recounting of the saga of Lady Fortune and Jeremy Dunster's decision to sell the animal. Having touched lightly upon Cressida's role in that choice, he dwelled on the reason why it could prejudice his lordship against Cressida as a companion for life.

"No finer sermon will ever be preached against the folly of gambling," said Amaryllis. She may have been unhappy for her poor friend, but she sounded righteous.

Torin found himself hoping that there would be no repercussions when he finally obtained permission from his elders to tell Amaryllis the dread secret of the Family Fleet.

"You can now appreciate the difficulty," he said at the end of a summary so concise that it would have won praise from any Q.C. who happened to overhear it.

"There is, however, something that *you* don't know." So saying, she proceeded to inform Torin about the advent of Kenneth Baldro, telling why she had called in the services of an alienist.

Torin sat back, stunned as if he had taken more blows at the hands of yet another addled Junior Conservative.

"I cannot see that the hiring of one of those people changes the situation in one way or another."

"I can!"

Torin blinked. He was beginning to understand the nightmare of a friend who had reported dreaming that he was holding a cricket bat in a game with rules that called for two thousand before an over.

"This situation, in my view," she continued, "merits a further consultation with him."

"What? Go to this Johnny again, this stranger, and talk to him about a family matter?"

"I have done so in the past for my friend's sake. For your sister's sake, I may add."

He did not point out that the results had been far from admirable. A young man raised with at least one sister acquires notable skills in the art and craft of rubbing along with females.

"You need have no fear about Mr. Baldro's discretion," Amaryllis said coolly. "Or his wisdom."

"Fear? Of course not."

"In that case, I will leave for Harley Street, and I hope that you are going to join me."

Torin concealed his difficulty in rising. "Only if we proceed by carriage."

"Certainly," said Amaryllis with the greatest possible sincerity. "I would not dream of disobeying an injunction of yours, dear, dear Torin."

Amaryllis told her story carefully, not hiding those feelings of sympathy that had brought her to seek further help for a friend in dire need. Her attitude had shifted in the last days, too, when it came to dealing with a friend. She felt strongly that the blessing of marriage should befall Cressida. If Cressida insisted upon plighting her troth with a horse dealer and reeling through life only a breath away from debtor's prison, so be it.

The serious-minded Baldro, having heard the problem put before him, sat back. His eyes were closed.

Torin, finally settled in a chair that offered some slight comfort, thought that the alienist had fallen asleep.

"You see?" he demanded of Miss Wyse. "There is no point in staying any longer."

Amaryllis put a finger to her lips. Unlike Torin, she was well aware that the great man was utilizing all his hard-won skills of ratiocination and deduction, to say nothing of keen analysis.

Mr. Baldro opened his eyes at last. He was looking at Torin. When he spoke, his tones were mildness itself.

"Would you by any chance recollect, Mr. Fleet, what foods you were served during the first few months of your life?"

Torin, wholly unnerved, admitted that the names had slipped his mind. Nor was there any way to find out.

"Ah, well then." The alienist was resigned to yet another instance in which he would obtain no help in formulating his theory of the sources of human behavior. Once it was published, colleagues were certain to concede his superiority. Admirers would truthfully say that before him all Vienna trembled. "The problem you bring me is a difficult one, but not without points of interest."

"You will, perhaps, confide in us," Torin suggested drily. If not for the difficult relations between Cressida and Dunster, he would have been in favor of staying home to learn the results of her second attempt to reach him on the telephone. It was unfortunate, in his view, that common sense had dictated otherwise.

"One point remains clear, as I see the matter," Baldro said firmly. "The good work that I have accomplished with Miss Fleet will go for naught if she pursues a man who races those animals. She must at all costs be kept from going to Coniston for a claiming-race at which the man will be present."

Torin saw the force of the argument for a reason other than Baldro's. "It would take main strength to keep her away."

"Instruct your father and mother to forbid her from taking the action."

Torin shook his head. "She will do whatever she decides is best, I assure you."

Baldro looked scandalized at the thought of some daughter disobeying her parents.

"Let them say that if she goes to Coniston, she will be unable to purchase new finery and will have no money to spend for a month."

Torin shook his head. It was regrettable that he couldn't possibly tell the alienist about Cressida's earnings keeping the family from attendance at suppers given by the Salvation Army to those who were destitute. Until he had obtained permission from his elders, he wouldn't be able to inform Amaryllis of that great truth, either.

"The goal I have indicated is the one that must be pursued," Baldro snapped, raising thick brows at the knowledge of anyone objecting to a solution he put forward. "I cannot tell you how to accomplish it by filling in every niggling little detail."

"Nevertheless," Torin began.

"You do not appreciate the full extent of the difficulty," Baldro interrupted in tones suitable for a mourner. "After her treatment is concluded, she would never marry a horseman. Till then, she is a prey to the blandishments of every racing course addict. Until her treatment is concluded, not only would she wed a trainer, but she would probably marry a horse."

Torin sat up, erect and angry. "I beg your pardon, sir!"

"I mean no disrespect to Miss Fleet or to yourself, sir. What I am saying is that Cressida Fleet is in a state in which her emotions become erratic. Part of her being wants to remain as she is, to stay an addict of gambling and the feverishness and uncertainty to which she is accustomed. In another part of her mind, however, seeing the possibility of breaking away from that odious habit, she wishes to experience a new freedom to the fullest. To be sure, her feelings shift between extremes. Is it any wonder that the young woman is torn by alternatives?"

Amaryllis had been listening with more than her usual intentness. The truth was being clearly pointed out by Baldro, the alienist to whom a human mind was an opened book.

"But what is to be done?" Amaryllis whispered.

"I have said that I cannot implement the minor details—no! I retract that. In this matter I have to make an exception. Would it be possible for Miss Fleet to visit my chambers before the day of the infamous claiming-race?"

"I will ask her to do so."

"Be firm."

"I will try to impress on her that the matter is urgent."

Torin looked from one to the other, dazed and unable to speak the few words that would resolve the particular difficulty.

"The race is to take place on Thursday, you tell me. Permit me to look at my engagement record for that day. Ah! I see that a Duke is due, and the wife of a Scottish peer, as well. Their appointments can be advanced by one day. A man of business is to have a first meeting on that afternoon, too. I should never have agreed to that. I will notify him that my client list is complete and suggest that he go elsewhere. Unless I have a choice, I should not spend time with a client who has no suitable connections."

Amaryllis waited tensely, leaning forward.

"As I see the situation, then, I had best travel to Coniston (in Cumberland or Lancashire, I believe, but somewhere in the Lake country) and speak to Miss Fleet once again at a racing course."

He did not add that he might well be seen doing so. Influential Sociables would be aware of his importance. To Torin, the addition was hardly necessary. To Amaryllis, it would have been merely distracting.

"But what can you do, then?"

"I shall remind Miss Fleet that she is under treatment by me and that she must follow my instructions. I will let her know, too, that I had not been able to instruct her further until I realized that the treatment was succeeding."

Torin was startled yet again. "What would those instructions be?"

"Simply that until she knows her mind by the conclusion of treatment, she must not marry." He suddenly drew out a pocket watch and inspected it gravely. "This has been most fruitful, but a client is due shortly, and we must endure a hiatus now."

Amaryllis did not turn to Torin until they had left Baldro's chambers at last. Her features were drawn.

"I'm sure that Mr. Baldro is right," she whispered. "In a perfect world, there would be no question of it. But if Cressida does not marry the one she desires, she may come to feel that it would be preferable to go through life as a spinster."

Torin agreed silently.

"Then what is to be done? Mr. Baldro is so definite, so sure of himself."

"I am convinced he will not be permitted to stand in Cressida's way," Torin responded, comfortable now that he had left the alienist's chambers. "You only know Cressida as a friend, but *I* know her as a sister."

CHAPTER TWENTY-SEVEN

Cressida had followed her brother's advice in embarking upon a course of action. She rushed to the telephone closet and made another effort to reach his lordship. This time, the gods looked upon her with favor. After a preliminary skirmish that involved Crouch, she heard Jeremy's unforgettably rich baritone voice in her ear.

"Cressida, I only returned moments ago," he said immediately, causing her to grip the receiver more firmly in hand so as to feel the vibrations of his tone. "Martyn, one of my tenants, was having trouble with a work horse and the matter wasn't resolved for hours. I've just received your message and was on the point of telephoning to you."

"I want to talk about Lady Fortune."

"Oh?" Was it her imagination or had his voice become a little cooler, a little more detached? "You may know that her recent record on the turf has convinced me that I was wrong about the animal's capacities. Even someone who has been tutored in the practical day-to-day matter of dealing with horses can apparently see less than a mere observer like yourself."

Convincing him of anything else about a horse, particularly that one, was going to be difficult. A gift for reasoning with another person had never been granted her. Knowing full well that she was so often right, she approached disagreements with a verbal blunderbuss. In dealing with Lord Jeremy Dunster, however, she would have to take the first of many exceptions.

"I understand that you have entered her in a claiming-race at Coniston, and that she is to be sold at auction immediately following."

"That is so."

"What I want you to do—what I *ask* you to do—is to withdraw the horse from that contest."

"You are suggesting, perhaps, that I keep her ladyship in my stable? What use could I have for a racehorse who runs poorly?"

"I don't know quite how to say this," Cressida admitted, "but I have come to realize that I might have been wrong about what you call 'her capacities.' "

"In this matter we have apparently changed sides," he rejoined irritably. Words about females and their irrationality seemed to be hovering on the telephone wire. "Let me remind you of what you yourself first made clear. Lady Fortune has run in such a fashion as to fall short of resounding victories."

"She could win, I think, if she was handled differently."

"What is it, might I ask, that convinced you along these lines? Intuition, perhaps?"

The suggestion was so nearly correct that she fell silent.

"I am pleased to have heard your voice once again," he said after a pause. "As for the advice you offer, I strongly disagree with it."

Cressida was impelled to warn, "If you dismiss Lady Fortune, you might be making the biggest mistake of your life."

He said formally, "I hope that we will see each other again in the future, the near future."

"In order to prove what I say about Lady Fortune," she insisted hurriedly, "all you have to do is to put her into a regular race with—"

In a softer voice, speaking over her words, Jeremy said that some work of his own remained to be done urgently. The connection between them was broken with gentleness, even regret.

Cressida was aware of the feeling for her person that had been shown. She was not, however, mollified. It would be necessary to take the family to Coniston and prove that his lordship was badly mistaken. The effort would have to be made behind Jemmy's back, for he would apparently not believe any pronouncement until the result was shown as a *fait accompli.*

Small wonder that she was muttering under her breath as she left the telephone closet. Her half-spoken words concerned the irrationality of men.

The guv'nor looked stunned when Torin had finished speaking. The two males had joined Mrs. Fleet in the study, which Cressida generally used for divining the results of races. Waiting for her to join them, all three seemed ill-at-ease.

"It was obvious that you would eventually wish to marry," the guv'nor said in a voice suitable for discussing the inevitability of old age and death. "What else is there to say?"

"Only that if Amaryllis is to be related to the family, she must be told about us."

The guv'nor winced. It meant that others would eventually know that the Fleet moneys were garnered by the efforts of a young female. The taint of gambling that surrounded these activities would be earnestly frowned on.

The guv'nor instructed solemnly, "Tell her the truth after the nuptials."

"That would be disreputable—pardon me, guv'nor, I didn't mean . . ."

Mrs. Fleet said, "One course strikes me as practical, if Mr. Fleet will agree, of course. First, let Amaryllis accept your offering for her. Then, after Sir Benedict Wyse has made dowry arrangements with us, inform her of the truth. In that way, the secret could be kept, as the Wyses wouldn't want it noised about, either."

The matter was still being discussed when Cressida walked in absently, her mind elsewhere.

"It shows great good sense on your part to marry rather than to be satisfied with an infatuation," Cressida said within moments after she had been apprised of the current agenda. "May you both be happy."

Only Mama noticed that Cressida, though genuinely pleased, had to force a smile of congratulation to her lips.

The proposal was made on Tuesday at a charity ball given by the Lord Mayor of London in the Guildhall. Almost as soon as Torin saw her again, he said that he loved her and wanted to marry and hoped that she reciprocated his strong feelings. He cursed himself even while speaking, convinced that his words ought to have been more formal, even florid.

"Of course I reciprocate," said Amaryllis promptly if shyly. "Shall we walk about in the night air?"

He wasn't able to embrace and kiss her in some privacy until they arrived at the porch. Under the City of London coat of arms with the motto *Domine Dirige Nos*, he more than made up for the tardiness that his previous impulsive act had forced on him.

A meeting took place on Wednesday afternoon at the chambers of Mortimer Cardew, Esq. Mr. Cardew, the solicitor for Sir Benedict Wyse and Lady Beryl, greeted his clients cheerily. In a more restrained manner, he bade welcome to Mr. and Mrs. Hartley Fleet.

The business of the meeting took up a surprisingly small amount of time. Each pair of elders formally agreed to place a sum of money in the hands of Mr. Cardew as trustee, for the benefit of Amaryllis and Torin. It was not mentioned that the amount to be contributed by the Fleets was smaller than what was offered by the other couple. Worthy of note was the fact that Mr. Hartley Fleet, generally considered to be under the well-kept thumb of his wife, spoke for both of them.

The ladies, who had been silent, waited until the last legal paper had been signed. At that point they busied themselves planning the words of that announcement that would appear in the *Times*. Mrs. Fleet and Lady Beryl started out by feigning a certain amount of geniality for each other, but their mutual absorption with the problem soon caused them to become genuinely cordial.

On Wednesday evening Torin began to feel the first intimations of worry. It suddenly occurred to him why his forthcoming engagement had truly made his elders uneasy.

He'd soon have to tell Amaryllis about the family secret, and it was possible that she might take the news badly. She might feel that the proposal had been made under false pretenses, that she'd be marrying into a family unworthy of hers. As a result she might decline not only to marry him, but ever to see him again.

He wasn't one to delay a duty, however, and made up his mind to tell all as soon as could be. He and Amaryllis were due to attend a reception tonight. The news could be broken to her in the carriage on their way over.

Amaryllis looked lovelier even than usual, which caused him further dismay. To be denied such a glorious sight for the balance of his life would be unbearable. Under a dark cloak she wore some garment in several shades of purple, considerably enhancing her figure. The effect on him was as devastating as his description would have been inadequate.

He spoke quickly and to the point once he started. Amaryllis was certainly surprised, her jaw dropping by several inches.

"And to think I never found that out," she said when he was done. She seemed bemused by no more than her inefficiency as a discoverer of information about others. As for those details of the family income, the sensible Amaryllis had taken that news lightly. She had already vowed to marry for love.

She suddenly gasped, though, and drew up a hand to a flushing cheek. "And I—I set Mr. Baldro to see to it that Cress gives up on her wagering. What must she have thought of me?"

"That you are a good friend."

"Heavens!" Then she burst out laughing at recollection of having shown her friendship unmistakably but so inappropriately.

Torin, listening, glowed with the knowledge that he had chosen a good-hearted girl to share his lot in life. The merriment proved contagious. By the time the carriage reached their destination, both were holding their sides.

CHAPTER TWENTY-EIGHT

There was good news for Cressida shortly after she and the family arrived at Coniston for the races. Only one claiming-race would be run, followed by an auction of the contenders, and that event would be last on the schedule. There was time to make her arrangements.

She put her trust in Torin. "I know that you are occupied with other matters, but there is something you must do for me."

"Of course," Torin agreed immediately, drawing his mind away from thoughts of the blessed Amaryllis. "What is it you need?"

"You must find the jockey who is to ride Lady Fortune today and send him up here so that I may talk to him."

"You could give me a message for the lad."

"No, I want him (and eventually Jemmy) to know the source who will be making it possible for them to enjoy added revenues."

Amaryllis appeared with her mother shortly after Torin's departure. The young women embraced, and congratulated each other on the knowledge that they would soon be in each other's families. Amaryllis was beautifully togged in royal blue, a full skirt edged at the hem with rows of narrow gold braid and striped diagonally by additional gold braid finished with tiny brass buttons. She could have passed for some member of a foreign army with a ladies' auxiliary.

"You look lovely," Cressida said with her usual sincerity. "Torin will be driven quite mad by your appearance."

"I certainly hope so," Amaryllis grinned in return, "else all the work will have been in vain."

Not until a few more exchanges had been completed did Amaryllis speak seriously. "You must know that Torin has told me all about your family situation. I do apologize for having inflicted Mr. Baldro upon you. I can imagine what you must have thought of me."

"I couldn't think of you in any way but kindly," Cressida said, "after balancing one consideration with another."

Amaryllis would have said the same about Cressida if she had shared her dear friend's direct disposition. Instead, she excused herself after a few moments and returned to Lady Beryl, who was waiting nearby.

Lady Beryl herself, smiling, approached Cressida as she resumed looking around impatiently for any sign of a jockey with the Dunster colors.

"I think it is so wonderful that you have learned all about horses," Lady Beryl said sincerely. She seemed close to awe at the notion of a female having acquired some skill associated with men, and only a few men at that.

Cressida responded as courteously as she could. In a corner of her mind, she knew now that she ought not to be surprised. Another woman wouldn't be censorious if that woman lived from the sweat of a man's brow.

"I wondered—ah, which horses you plan to bet upon today," the older woman said shyly.

"Only the last race interests me here, Lady Beryl, and I am depending on a meeting before I venture money upon Lady Fortune."

"I thought that one of the horses I saw only a few moments ago looked so striking that I would show my confidence in his prowess by venturing a guinea."

Cressida shrugged at the prospect.

"Further, his name is Lucky Groom, which I do think is an omen."

Cressida took more time to look along the stands. She was occupied in that manner when Lady Beryl resumed her discourse.

"I have always been very fond of the hurdle races, my dear. Perhaps you could be persuaded to join me at such an event."

An answer was required. "I will do it gladly if the racing does not occur at a time when I must occupy myself with family matters."

"Oh, I felt sure you would instruct me which of the steeds to wager upon. There would be a gain for you as well as me."

Cressida shook her head firmly. "I only bet on flat races, Lady Beryl. The others are too risky. Hurdles introduce a factor that cannot be reckoned in advance. Worst of all, the riders are not players (so to speak) but gentlemen. That makes it far more difficult to know if a given rider will rise above some fresh difficulty to offer a good race."

Lady Beryl was nonplused. "That is very interesting," she said vaguely, but not as if she was convinced.

Cressida felt relieved when Amaryllis walked off with her mama. She remained free to look about. It hardly seemed to matter. By the end of the second race, there was no sign of a jockey in the stands.

"Am I addressing Mr. Baldro?"

"Yes, sir, you are."

"The alienist?"

"Indeed." Baldro would have liked to hear "celebrated" between the other's last two words, but the recognition from a cultivated stranger was satisfying.

"You were accurately described to me," said the newcomer, glancing down without expression at the alienist's Norfolk jacket of no color but black. "I am Hartley Fleet."

"You are the father of Miss Cressida, of course." Baldro couldn't make the effort to smile, but he did incline his head.

"My daughter's friend, Miss Amaryllis Wyse, has told me why you are here."

"I trust that my service to this date has been satisfactory." Baldro waited for the compliment that would follow.

It was not forthcoming.

"I regret that you have been acting under a series of misunderstandings," said Cressida Fleet's father. "My daughter has no need to see you. Should you so much as speak to her today, you will be disturbing her at a time of great importance in her life. I beg, therefore, that you do not go near her."

"But I came to continue offering my professional help!" Baldro protested. "The treatment is at a stage where it must not be broken off."

"Properly speaking, sir, there is no treatment."

"If this message is coming directly from your daughter, Mr. Fleet, she must be asked why she has taken such a step. By what ulterior motive is she impelled to do so?"

"I can but inform you again that you have been the unwitting victim of a series of misunderstandings, which I regret. If you send me a due bill, because of the circumstances, a remittance will be sent in the next post. By disregarding these instructions, however, and attempting to make contact with my daughter, you would make it certain that no honorarium will ever be paid by me. I bid you a good day."

Mr. Hartley Fleet adopted a dignified pace in leaving.

Before that visition, Baldro had been enjoying the afternoon. It offered the best of June weather with not too much sun and hints of lazy warmth to follow. These conditions allowed for the best possible display of finery as worn by socially prominent improvers of the breed. Mr. Baldro had briefly renewed acquaintance with a former steward of the Jockey Club. Not only had the latter deigned to return his greetings, but had offered a brief reminiscence of Admiral John Henry Rous, who had been affectionately known as "The Dictator of the Turf" and was dead these twenty years. It could not be denied that on this very special day Kenneth Baldro was rubbing elbows with the socially mighty of the Empire.

His spirits had just been dampened, however. Experience came to his rescue, reminding him of relatives who had been opposed to any change in a daughter, even one that was obviously for the better. His first step would be to make sure that Miss Cressida Fleet's true feelings were reflected in the recent *ukase* that had been handed down. For which purpose, the best source of information was his client's friend.

Miss Amaryllis Wyse was in conversation with an older woman, who turned out to be her mother. A brief introduction was required, although the alienist's impatience for a ceremony at this time must have been clear. Indeed, Miss Wyse, with suitable apologies, soon led him a few paces beyond the older woman's earshot.

"I can now assure you that no treatment for a difficulty caused by racing will be of the slightest use," Miss Wyse said after the question had been put bluntly.

"But Miss Fleet was making enormous progress! It must be that she herself is frightened of the alterations that will be wrought in her when I have freed her at last from her obsession."

"Mr. Baldro, I regret that I cannot tell you more without violating a confidence."

The alienist didn't feel that she had raised an impassable barrier. He was on the point of snapping that he wasn't going to endure *this* hiatus.

There was an interruption. A young woman paused to greet Miss Wyse and spoke a few words. Miss Wyse took advantage of the new situation to dislodge herself from Baldro's company, but not until she had courteously introduced Miss Letitia Waghorn.

Rather than follow Amaryllis Wyse, who almost certainly wouldn't stir from her mother's side for another private talk, he looked around in hopes of seeing Miss Cressida Fleet. Perhaps the sight of him in turn might move her to take the correct path in order to make sure of her future happiness.

The girl to whom he had been introduced remained in front of him. She was smiling hopefully, expecting his attention to return. Miss Waghorn was a dark-haired and comely young woman dressed in white. If she looked sickly, that would be of small import to a man who would be considered as a fount of medical knowledge.

Something else had occurred to him. "Would you be the daughter of Sir Frederick Waghorn? Ah! I had anticipated being consulted by him during the day, but I prefer to consult with his daughter instead."

Miss Waghorn dimpled prettily, as he had expected. Attractive and amiable as she was, his attention was caught in the main by the recollection that her mama was trying to enhance the family position among the Sociables by doing much for charity. A man did have to take himself a wife after all, and an alienist wanting a practice among the titled could do far worse than to link himself with the family Waghorn.

It crossed his mind only afterward that Sir Frederick and Lady Dorothy might want to help a son-in-law in ways other than those that seemed obvious. They could advance his stature immeasurably after marriage by being forthcoming with him about the foods that Miss Waghorn (Letitia, as he dared to think of her) had eaten during her infancy. Eventually, too, they could persuade friends to be of assistance as well. He would be on the way to proving the validity of his theory, to having his first paper on the subject published, perhaps to gaining a title himself.

Miss Waghorn had joined her mama at the races. An introduction was affected between the older woman and the alienist. Baldro found her intelligent and aware that her daughter's merits, numerous as these were, might not suit every eligible bachelor. It was time to indicate that his interest in the young woman could very well grow.

"Tell me, Miss Waghorn," he asked, for once thinning his lips in an unforced smile, "do you come to the races often?"

Cressida could have prepared a long list of reasons for not liking the course at Coniston. For one, it had been laid out with some sharp corners, making for greater difficulties in predicting the performance of a given contestant. Nor was it one of those areas to which gamblers applied the celebrated maxim, "Horses for Courses"; no animal liked Coniston well enough to win here whenever it ran. Worst of all, she and the family had lost money there on two consecutive occasions back in '96.

It didn't surprise her in this mood that only club members could achieve access to the enclosure near the finish line. She didn't want to pay a fresh fee to get in every time it struck her fancy to look there in the search for Torin and some infernal jockey who rode for Jemmy.

It was only a matter of time before she saw her brother again, his firm chin tilted as if to guide him. More and more he was coming to look a younger and more aggressive version of one of Mama's Castle relations.

Nor was she entirely surprised to see a small young man near him, a young man clothed in the Dunster colors of red and white. Torin's mission had been crowned with success.

She did not, however, expect to see the figure striding to the right of the jockey. She couldn't help recognizing him at first sight, of course. A female of even the smallest intelligence would have known immediately that the next minutes were going to be rather difficult.

CHAPTER TWENTY-NINE

The white silk bodice of Cressida's fawn-shot poplinette walking gown was quivering as if under its own power by the time he faced her. In his preoccupation, the phenomenon escaped his notice.

"It is no more than reasonable for me to want to know," he began a little heavily, "why you wish to speak with Osmay here."

"It is about the horse."

"I had guessed that much. You have, I assume, evolved some plan to make certain that Lady Fortune wins."

"I cannot absolutely promise that much."

"What then, if I may ask further?"

"I think I can promise that her performance will improve over what it has been in the recent past. You will clearly see her once again as a horse with winning possibilities."

"And how are you planning to do this? Will you mesmerize the beast by holding her with a stern and glittering eye while you instruct her to make her mind a blank?"

Because she was angrily breathing even faster, one of the paste buttons fell from the right-side epaulette of the walking gown. She didn't move toward it or show the slightest regret.

"Well, Miss Fleet? I can truthfully tell you that I am all ears to find out just how you plan to accomplish the miracle."

The sarcasm caused her to flush and then adopt an action that she would later find surprising.

"I will amend what I have previously said. Your diplomatic

behavior causes me to insist that I will speak only to Mr. Osmay here and tell him what it is that must be done."

Jemmy Dunster flushed.

"Further, I will put you on your word not to inquire what step is being taken until the race has been concluded and Lady Fortune's performance can be assessed."

"You can't ask me to accept that!"

Torin, who had been listening, spoke with his mother's practicality. "You want to observe the possibilities for improving the performance of a horse for which you have no hopes, Lord Dunster. If she does badly here, you will gain little or nothing from the auction that is to follow the last race. It behooves you, therefore, to accept my sister's terms."

"No, it does not. Let me say again, as I have said to her in the past, that I haven't the slightest confidence in her day-to-day knowledge of horses and how to deal with them."

Cressida had never done anything more difficult than keeping her lips compressed at this time. Every nerve in her body was urging her to tell all, to impart the secret immediately. Her silence was an indication that instead of always demanding that actions be taken according to her preferences, she could consider somebody else's views with respect. By the same token, if he would agree to the terms there was hope that his occasionally stubborn convictions might be open to change.

"I am running a different horse in the fifth race and Osmay is riding," he said brusquely. "There is no time for these parleys, in any case."

Cressida looked away, feeling his eyes rest thoughtfully upon her.

He was giving a massive shrug when she looked up. "Very well, very well. My expectations for Lady Fortune are low in any case. Let me see what will happen if she runs according to the preferences of a dilettante."

He turned to leave. Watching him stride with longer steps than usual, Cressida nervously touched a section of the gold embroidery at her waist. There was a loose thread. If that wasn't repaired at home, the gold and spangles would eventually unravel. It seemed as if her gown was falling apart at the rate of one feature every few minutes.

Torin suddenly said, "There are some secrets that other mortals aren't meant to know."

He turned away. Most likely he had discovered the current whereabouts of Amaryllis. There was no reason to waste time with a mere sister.

Cressida addressed herself to the jockey. "Is the horse in good condition?"

"Yes, Miss," said Osmay. He was a ferret-faced man in the twenties, with small eyes that probed briskly in every direction. He might have been a general inspecting the terrain on which he is going to fight a battle. "Her ladyship is larky and hungry. Her coat has shine enough to reflect the gold teeth on a bookmaker."

"But she'll be carrying a weight into the race, an added weight beside you." Cressida hadn't previously taken that into consideration, which would have been enough to prove that she wasn't herself. "Does an added weight always bother her?"

"No more than everything else seems to, Miss, when she's on the oval."

"Good." Cressida leaned forward and spoke quietly. "Now here is what has to be done."

The jockey gave her succeeding words his fullest attention. Those normally small eyes grew wider in admiration when she was finished.

"Is it possible that nothin' else has been wrong with her all this time and I never twigged it and neither did Lord Dunster or any of the lads? Could it be as simple as that?"

"I think there's a very good chance I'm right, and the chance is worth taking."

" 'Strewith it is!" the jockey breathed, and lapsed further into the *patois* of that district from which he hailed. "Cor lumme, stone the crows!"

Cressida took this latter as an expression of admiration for her.

Torin said calmly, "If Cressy marries in the near future, I will have to take over by deciding which horses the family should bet upon."

Amaryllis agreed with a reservation. "For a while I suppose you would."

"What does that mean, dear, 'for a while'?"

"I spoke to my papa about your situation, love. He was somewhat disappointed that you aren't wealthy, but he feels that any man with a skill must find a way to capitalize upon it to the maximum."

"How does he suggest I do so?"

"Papa says that at first you have to walk before you can run."

Torin snorted. "With weights, presumably. Like a horse."

"No, what he suggests is that from now on you begin to write for one of the racing papers. Your essays would predict which horses are likely to win at important races. Papa has enough influence to see that you are permitted to do so. If you are successful, you will acquire a reputation as a seer in these matters, and that will be all you need to obtain financing from him to start a racing paper of your own. That is what you have wanted to do."

"Yes, of course, I see that now." Torin felt like a traveler lost in the dark and who is made aware of the coming of dawn.

"You will have to keep a schedule," she warned, "whether you want to or not."

"I can accept difficulties in stride if only I am doing work that I like," he said easily. "Marriage to you, for example, will not be work, of course, but no major difficulties will be offered, either, in keeping to any schedule that may be necessary."

"And I," said Amaryllis, grinning from ear to ear, "will always think of you as my bettor half."

Torin winced at the pun. Just as the crowd's attention became fixed on the running of the fifth race, he took Amaryllis in his arms and brought his lips down to hers.

Mr. and Mrs. Fleet were taking their ease in the stands while they waited for the claiming race to get under way.

"I don't see Torin," said Mr. Fleet after a long look around.

"He is with Amaryllis and probably her mama, too," Mrs. Fleet responded. "That woman hangs on to Amaryllis like a leech. Our son hasn't lost one family, but has gained an albatross."

"I suppose that Amaryllis will put a stop to that situation as soon as the marriage vows have been taken," Mr. Fleet said pacifically.

"That sort of situation is not easy. You can surely recall what problems were caused for us by the continual presence of my maiden Aunt Genevieve in the first weeks of our marriage."

"But you prevailed, my dear."

They were joined by Cressida, who had been watching the fifth race by herself. She had been well aware that Jemmy would be watching keenly, too, and the gesture had an effect of making her feel closer to him.

"I am glad that Lord Dunster's horse won it," said Mr. Fleet, who had noticed the high point of the recent equine set-to.

"Not only did Society Scandal win, but it didn't happen by default as at Hexham," Cressida pointed out, settling herself beside Mama.

"Certainly that should put him into a better mood," Mama said shrewdly.

Cressida was gloomy. "I doubt if he will remain in a pleasant mood for long."

"The man is addled," Mr. Fleet said irritably and loyally. "Imagine a young chap with the opportunity to marry Cressy and hesitating about it for even a moment."

"Papa, you are kindness itself," said his daughter, smiling with as much agony as Mr. Kenneth Baldro at his grimmest. "In the teeth of the sort of difficulty he has been poising, I am frank to admit that I may not want to marry *him.*"

"I wouldn't be surprised," Mr. Fleet agreed, nodding fiercely.

Mama, of course, was not persuaded of her daughter's temporary honesty. "I have seen you near Dunster, Cressy. If he made the offer and was rejected out of hand, I'd be astonished."

"I don't think he will make the offer," Cressida said grimly. "He will never admit that I have any knowledge whatever of the turf and will be badly offended when he knows otherwise, even if that is of advantage to him."

Mr. Fleet began, "But you must tell him—" He halted.

Cressida was quick to take advantage of the opening. "He will never begin to understand my claims to expertise along that line until the reason for it is made crystal clear."

The elder Fleets exchanged glances.

"All London will know sooner or later," said Mr. Fleet, cut to the bone. "Someone who has access to the secret will tell another and so on. I will be a laughingstock when I next have to pay my yearly subscription at the Alpine Club. And I say nothing of the Turf, the Thatched House, the United Whist, the Cocoa Tree, and the St. George's Chess."

"They're approaching!" Cressida called out, looking down to the horses on their way to the starting point.

Mr. Fleet inspected the racing paper he had brought with him. "Good heavens! I see that Overweening Ambition is in the race to be claimed."

"She won at Llandrindod Wells," Mama recalled fondly. "Everyone in Wales on that day was astonished. Everyone but Cressy."

"And here is Arrogant Baroness, too."

"She is suitable to pull a London growler," Cressida said, having misjudged that animal at Berwick-on-Tweed. She was straining her eyes in peering down. "I don't see *her.*"

"And Insolent Maiden-in-Waiting, as well," Mr. Fleet said, having resumed his reading.

"A good horse if she had a more understanding owner," Cressida said. "Sir Miles Pleydell-Bouverie may not mistreat his animals, but he doesn't get the best out of them, either."

"A haughty group," Mama remarked, having considered the various names.

"And here is Morganatic Marriage," Mr. Fleet said. "A splendid animal on which I would probably want to wager."

"No, it's Lady Fortune's race if she's been correctly done by," Cressida said. "There she is!"

The animal looked no different to her eyes. Lady Fortune was moving swiftly, but whether as the result of irritation or high spirits it was impossible to tell. Cressida raised the glasses that she had borrowed from Mama. It was impossible to be sure whether the jockey, Osmay, had been permitted to follow the instructions he had been painstakingly given.

"It does not look excessively promising," Mr. Fleet pointed out after the start.

Lady Fortune was running fifth. Cressida had expected the animal to take her top speed almost from the start.

Mama pointed out, "The first turn is coming up, and might make a difference."

It did, but not enough of one. Lady Fortune moved past Insolent Maiden-in-Waiting, who wouldn't be heard from again on this afternoon.

She overtook Arrogant Baroness on the straight. Making for the rail, which she rode against, she was approaching Morganatic Marriage, who was four lengths ahead.

"Only four lengths," Cressida whispered, and realized that her free hand was making a fist. "There is still reason for hope."

Lady Fortune was running even with Overweening Ambition. The jockeys could very possibly have shaken hands.

It was Overweening Ambition who pulled away, causing Cressida to pound her lap with the fist. Didn't Lady Fortune realize that the stakes in this race were her own future as well as Jemmy's? Why was the animal dawdling?

Mama made no further prediction until Lady Fortune once more pulled even with Overweening Ambition.

"She is coiling herself up to make her move," Mama said, leaning forward. It was rare for her to show interest in a race on which the family hadn't wagered, but Lady Fortune's performance was striking.

"I certainly hope—yes, you're right."

Lady Fortune had moved like a shell from its cannon. She left Overweening Ambition behind and drew close to Morganatic Marriage's tail. More than one onlooker rose excitedly and started to cheer the contenders.

"I do like Morganatic Marriage," Papa said perversely. "As a horse, I mean, Cressy. I understand the reasons for your strong feeling otherwise, but she is so beautiful to see."

Cressida hardly heard. Slowly but surely, Lady Fortune drew even with the other horse. She was suddenly ahead by a nose, then by head and neck, then by half her body. Lady Fortune simply wouldn't tolerate any outcome but victory. It seemed that Osmay had sensed the horse's great reserves of energy and permitted Lady Fortune to make her own race in the main. He hadn't used the whip at all. Nothing would have been more unnecessary.

Cressida sat back wearily after the last cheer, stirred so deeply that she was on the verge of crying. In and of itself it was the sort of athletic event that had first attracted her to racing. Only the call of need, the urgency for making bets, had caused her to forget that a race could be deeply moving. She had a strong feeling that she would never again entirely lose that special memory.

"I have made my point with his lordship," she said after a moment to catch her breath. "I think he will come to regard me as an ally and even more than that."

"Yes," Papa said carefully, turning to look at his wife.

"Your papa feels as I do," said Mama, taking it upon herself once more to speak for both of them. "You should tell his lordship the truth about your family. Like Torin and his Amaryllis, though, I feel you should do so only after Jemmy makes the offer for your hand in marriage."

That attitude was not, after all, unexpected. Cressida agreed quickly and rose to find his lordship. She would congratulate him on the outcome of the race, then wait for his effusive remarks.

For she had no doubt that he appreciated her perceptiveness and his words would reflect a certain awe. No doubt his eyes would gleam admiringly. In sum, he would be entranced, a willing captive to her intelligence. And to her charm.

She proceeded toward the enclosure, prepared to pay the admission. Certainly Jemmy would be there among friends.

Along the way she happened to catch sight of Kenneth Baldro. The alienist was deep in conversation with Letitia Waghorn, of all people. Cressida felt pleased for both of them. She had given no thought to Baldro today and hoped that the pleasure of Letitia's acquaintance would console him when Amaryllis discreetly let him know that one certain name must disappear from his roster of clients.

She found Jeremy in the enclosure. Her heart pounded a little more quickly at sight of him. He was looking around avidly. Hoping to see her, Cressida had no doubt.

Nothing loath, she walked over immediately.

He did smile at sight of her, but only for a moment. "You were very clever about the horse, and I intend to learn how you knew what had to be done and what it was that you persuaded Osmay to do."

"Why aren't you finding out at this moment? I will be only too happy to tell you."

"First, I have to discover Osgood's whereabouts."

"I—beg your pardon?"

"Surely you recall my wealthy friend, the Honorable Osgood Nisbet?"

"I met him in Cheshire shortly after I met you, but it is beside the point. Why must you seek him out now of all times?"

"My dear Cressida." His smile showed an appreciation of her feeling that other matters were of greater importance. "Your almost occult intelligence in the matter of Lady Fortune has created what I may call a difficulty."

Yet another difficulty! "Please explain this in the fewest possible words."

"As you know, with the race over, Lady Fortune must be sold. I have no choice in consenting to that."

"I do understand it is the major condition for being permitted to enter a horse in a claiming-race."

"Her performance has convinced me all over again that I was originally right to feel she is capable of great achievements."

"Certainly it has convinced you."

"What I want Osgood to do is to buy her and pay for her, then turn her over to me."

"That makes sense." Cressida cocked her head inquiringly. "But I am under the strong impression that you dread doing so."

"I don't have a ready call upon the necessary money, and I know that Osgood will set a price for the service. He may well charge more than I can easily afford."

"I will never understand a gentleman's idea of friendship," Cressida said. She was smiling now. "But you may not need the services of the ostensibly honorable Mr. Nisbet."

"Do you mean that your father would make the purchase at your request?"

"The Fleet family would have to think twice about buying stirrup leather, for reasons which I feel strongly I will very soon be able to make clear."

Although his brows were raised in surprise, Dunster resumed looking around for his friend.

"For your own sake, Jeremy, I ask that you not enter in any decisive agreement with Mr. Nisbet until I return."

"Very well, if you are quick. But what do you think you can do—?"

"It would take too much time to tell you what is on my mind."

She had no trouble finding Amaryllis. Her future sister-in-law was in Torin's company and that of her mother, Lady Beryl. She and the others were also in the presence of the Fleet elders.

"If you do me a favor, Amaryllis, you will get back the money you expend, should you decide you want it. Or you might prefer that your purchase make a superb, an unforgettable wedding present for Jeremy and myself."

And instantly, as a friend should, Amaryllis asked, "What is it that you want me to do?"

CHAPTER THIRTY

She told him about the arrangement as soon as she returned to his presence. Jeremy had shown confidence in her by remaining in place.

"That leaves one more matter open to immediate discussion," he said as soon as he had expressed gratitude for her having acted. "What did you tell Osmay to do in the first place to make Lady Fortune into a winner?"

"I knew that she was a horse who slipped her tongue over the bit, a gesture that can shut off some of a horse's needed air during a race," Cressida said. "The solution, of course, was simply to tie down her tongue before she ran. You see the result."

"But how could you 'know' that she slipped her tongue over the bit? You can't ever have seen her that closely from a position on the racecourse."

She had to think. "Now that you ask I recall that I did see her closely at your estate in Shropshire. After a workout, she started to take on."

"And everybody thought she had a preference for histrionics," he admitted ruefully. "Rather than using intuition, you reasoned from observation at first-hand. You've proved my point and you're blessedly incapable of telling a lie to win some argument."

In the face of his praise, Cressida was wise to be silent and let him continue.

"It is no wonder that I have loved you for every second since the race at Cheshire."

Cressida asked weakly, "Are you making an offer for my hand in marriage?"

"I am demanding your hand in marriage, darling Cressida."

"I accept," she said immediately. "Now I must tell you about my family and—"

"Tell me your sordid tale some other time." He came closer to seal the agreement.

Cressida wasn't surprised that several more of the white buttons popped off her walking gown at the press of his body against hers.

She drew back her head unwillingly and recalled another man's words of temporary dismissal. "We must endure a hiatus now."

"What? I never heard such nonsense!"

And, ignoring the murmurs on all sides, he emphasized those words by his next deed.